More & More
TALES TO GIVE YOU
Goosebumps®

Look for more GOOSEBUMPS books
by R.L. Stine:

More & More
TALES TO GIVE YOU
Goosebumps®
TEN SPOOKY STORIES
R.L. STINE

AN
APPLE
PAPERBACK

SCHOLASTIC INC.
New York   Toronto   London   Sydney   Auckland

A PARACHUTE PRESS BOOK

ISBN 0-590-23796-9

12 11 10 9 8 7 6 5 4 3 2 1   7 8 9/9 0 2/0

Printed in the U.S.A.

First Scholastic Printing, May 1997

CONTENTS

THE HAUNTED GUITAR

"I am *not* lazy, Beth. I work hard."

"Yeah. Right, Jeffrey." My friend Beth rolled her eyes. "You work really hard — figuring out the easiest way to do things."

"That's not lazy, Beth. That's smart!" I laughed.

"Smart?" Beth wrinkled her freckled nose. "Weeding the garden with a vacuum cleaner is not smart, Jeffrey."

Okay. I admit it. That wasn't one of my best ideas. I mean, it worked great on the weeds. Sucked them right up. The problem was — it sucked up the rest of the garden too. All the dirt. And most of the tulips.

"We'd better hurry." Beth peered up at the thick black clouds rolling in. "It's going to start pouring any minute."

It was late afternoon. Heavy clouds gathered above us, turning the sky dark as night. The street lamps flickered on.

1

Beth and I had just left the post office. My mom sent us there to pick up a package for her.

A brisk wind started to blow. The brim of my baseball cap flew up. I tucked my mom's package under my arm. Then I tugged my baseball cap down hard over my forehead.

"Can't you walk any faster?" Beth complained. "I hate this part of town. It's really creepy here."

It *is* kind of creepy here, I thought, glancing up and down the street. We were in the old section of town. Most of the stores closed when the new mall opened last year.

I spotted a scraggly gray cat up ahead. It darted across the road and disappeared into a dark alley.

The rest of the street was deserted.

Beth turned the corner and broke into a jog.

"Hey, Beth. Wait. Look at this!"

I stopped in front of a burned-out store. A heavy blanket of black soot coated its red bricks.

It hadn't started raining yet, but water dripped from the store's roof. Water from fire hoses.

Whoa. We just missed the fire, I thought, watching the running water. It poured down the front of the building, then into a sewer.

I stared up at the store's charred sign. I could still read the burned words: SAL'S MUSIC STORE.

In the blackened window I could make out a

drum set and two electric guitars. What was left of them, that is. They looked as if they had melted on the spot.

A bolt of lightning suddenly sliced through the sky. The bright flash lit up the inside of the store. Wow. What a mess.

All the instruments inside, the walls, the counters, the music books, everything — totally burned up.

"Come on, Jeffrey. Let's go." Beth walked over to me, struggling against a strong gust of wind. She tugged hard on my arm. "I hate lightning."

"Okay. Okay," I told her. "In a second." I pushed against the front door. It creaked opened. "First — let's check out the store."

"We can't go in there!" Beth shouted. "The ceiling could come crashing down — on our heads!"

"Don't be such a wimp," I said, walking inside.

Beth stomped into the store behind me.

It was almost totally dark inside. And totally wet. The floor was still warm from the fire. I could feel the heat rise up through my sneakers.

An eerie stillness settled in the smoky room.

Water trickled down the walls. Dripped lightly from the ceiling. From the high shelves.

Curls of smoke hung in the air. My eyes started to burn.

I glanced around the store. The fire had destroyed everything. Everything.

In one corner of the room, the electric keyboards stood in a puddle of water — their white keys scorched black by the flames.

Charred, wrecked violins and flutes lay scattered on the floor, eaten by the fire.

Flakes of ash — like black snow — drifted in the air. Then fluttered to the floor.

I listened to the light drip, drip, drip of the water.

I listened to the creaking shelves, heavy with moisture, buckling under the weight.

"I can't breathe," Beth said, coughing. "And it's too creepy in here. I want to go. Now."

"Okay. Okay," I said. I walked over to a pile of guitars on the floor. Their necks were twisted and shriveled — melted by the heat of the fire.

"My dad was going to bring me here to pick out a guitar," I told Beth. "But, look — the guitars are all burned black."

"I want to go. NOW!" Beth insisted. "If we get caught in here, we'll be in major trouble."

"Hey! What's that?" I pointed to a shelf at the back of the store.

"Jeffrey, I'm going to leave without you," Beth declared.

I ignored her and headed for the back. There, on a corner shelf, stood an old, wooden guitar. Covered with soot.

I brushed it clean with my shirtsleeve. Then I studied it, turning it around and around.

"Beth, can you believe this?" I said, running my thumb over the strings. The notes echoed softly in the smoky room. "It's the only instrument in the store that's not ruined."

"It's just a crummy old guitar, Jeffrey. Let's go!" Beth headed toward the door.

"Okay. I'm coming. Maybe I'll take it home," I said, staring down at the guitar. "No one will miss it."

"You can't do that!" Beth spun around. "That's *stealing*!"

"They'll probably just throw it out anyway," I argued. "I'm sure it's water damaged or something."

"It doesn't matter. It's still stealing," Beth said. "You know that. Why are you taking it?"

"Because it's here. It's easier than waiting for my dad to buy me one. No one will ever know."

"You always want to do things the easy way. It's going to get you in big trouble, Jeffrey. Really." Beth shook her head.

Yeah, right, I thought. How could taking an old crummy guitar get me in trouble?

"Where did you get that guitar?" I met Dad on the steps as I headed up to my room.

"Uh . . . well . . . a friend loaned it to me," I lied.

"Great. Now you can see if you like playing it — before I buy you one." Dad clapped me on the back.

I went into my bedroom and sat down on the bed. I ran my fingers over the guitar. Over the old wood — scratched and worn. But when I strummed it, it made a nice, mellow sound.

I crossed the room and leaned the guitar in a corner.

I should sign up for lessons tomorrow, I thought as I headed downstairs for dinner.

That's what I'll do. I'll go to the music studio in town and sign up for lessons. No — maybe I should wait until next week.

I'll have to think more about this, I decided. That's what I'll do — I'll think about it.

"Lazy. Lazy. Lazy." Beth's words echoed in my head as I tried to fall asleep that night.

After dinner I called her — for the answers to our math homework. She gave them to me — but she said I was the laziest person on earth.

I sat up and fluffed my pillow.

The house was dark and silent. Mom and Dad had already dozed off. But I was having trouble falling asleep.

It isn't lazy to take a few shortcuts, I told myself. I pulled the blanket up to my chin. Beth is wrong. She's definitely wrong.

I finally drifted off to sleep . . . until I heard the music.

Huh?

I sat up in bed. I rubbed my eyes. I listened.

There it was again. Guitar music.

Where is it coming from? Am I dreaming? I wondered.

I stared across my dark room.

Whoa! The music floated from the corner. A soft blues riff.

How could that be?

My heart began to thud in my chest.

I swung my legs out of bed. They shook as my feet touched the floor.

I crept across the room — and gasped.

A man sat on a stool in the corner of my room. He was playing the guitar.

My stomach tightened as I stared at him. He wore a tattered blue sweater and faded jeans. His dark brown face was lined with wrinkles. His hair, rimmed with gray.

I listened to the music — a beautiful, haunting melody. The old man continued to play. He didn't seem to see me.

"How — how did you get in here?" I finally managed to choke out. "What are you doing here?"

The man kept playing. But he gazed into my eyes. "You took my guitar," he said in a hushed voice.

"Well . . . y-yes," my voice cracked. My hands began to shake. "I'm s-sorry. I didn't know it was yours. You can take it back."

"I can't," the man replied.

7

"Why not?" I asked, confused.

"Because I'm dead," he answered.

I gasped in horror. "You're joking — right? I'm going to have to call my dad —"

"You probably never heard of me. I'm Memphis Willy. And this is Gertie, my guitar. Gertie and I traveled some long roads together. We played a lot of blues."

Willy kept playing. His body rocked gently in time with the music. His left foot softly tapped out the rhythm. His head swayed from side to side.

"I can't stop playing, see," he said in his quiet voice. "Gertie and I were together so long. Even after I died, I couldn't stop playing. I love the music so much . . . I can't stop. I could *never* stop. . . ."

"Well, it sounds great," I told him. "I mean, I wish I could play like that. But you have to go. If you wake up my parents, how will I explain? Here. Follow me. I'll show you the front door."

"Don't need a door." Willy shook his head. "Don't need any doors since I died. You say you want to play like this?"

Willy shoved the guitar into my hands. "Here. Give it a try," he said.

"I — I don't know how," I protested. "You have to go. Really."

"I'll show you," Willy insisted. "Go ahead. Put your fingers on the frets. Tell you what . . . we'll play a little blues. I'll help you."

I wanted this guy out of here. Maybe if I play a little, he'll leave, I decided.

I placed the fingers of my left hand on the neck of the guitar.

I rested my right thumb on the strings.

And then — I started to play.

I was playing music!

I was playing the blues — just like Memphis Willy!

"Hey! How are you doing that? You're moving my fingers!" I cried.

"Yeah. See how easy it is," Willy said. "I can make you the best blues guitarist on earth!"

Whoa. I plucked the strings. My left hand ran up and down the guitar neck. The music flowed from my fingers!

I was really playing the blues!

No lessons!

No practicing!

I was great!

"Sounds good, kid," Willy said. "Want to be partners? Want to keep playing? Want to be my *living* partner?"

"Will I be able to play like this all the time?" I asked excitedly.

"Yeah," Willy answered. "All the time."

What a shortcut! Wait till Mom and Dad hear this! Wait till Beth sees how great I am!

I can't believe she told me not to take the guitar. What a moron!

"I'll be your partner!" I said.

I was thrilled! Totally thrilled. My fingers kept moving. Kept making this wonderful music!

"It's a deal, partner," Willy said.

I gazed up at him — and he started to fade away.

Whoa! My eyes grew wide as Willy continued to fade. I — I don't believe this! He really is a ghost!

My fingers continued to play. A sweet blues riff filled the room. "Are you still here, Willy?" I called out. "Are you still here?"

No answer.

I kept playing.

My fingers began to move a little faster. The music sounded awesome.

Better stop now, I thought. Don't want to wake Mom and Dad. But wait till I show everyone in the morning. They are not going to believe this!

I tried to stop playing.

But my fingers kept moving.

"Uh . . . Willy? I've got to go to sleep now. I don't want to wake my parents. Willy — are you here?"

No answer.

I tried to stop playing. I tried to put the guitar down. But I couldn't. Some kind of force held it in place.

My fingers kept moving.

"Hey — what's going on, Willy?" My voice shook. "I've got to stop now. Willy?"

I walked over to the bed. Tried to set the guitar down on it. But my arms wouldn't budge. The guitar rested snug against my chest.

I broke out into a cold sweat.

My fingers kept playing.

I tried to uncurl them.

I tried to release my grip.

"Oh, no!" I can't control them at all, I realized.

I took a deep breath — and tried to toss the guitar on the floor.

I tried again and again. But the harder I tried, the tighter my fingers pressed down on the strings.

Fingers pressing. Moving up and down.

Playing. Playing. Playing the blues.

"Ow!" My fingertips burned now.

My temples began to pound.

"Where are you, Willy?" I cried. "I need your help!"

Willy didn't answer.

I kept playing.

"Come on — Willy," I begged. "I have to stop! My fingers are really hurting me. I'm getting blisters."

Over the sound of the music, Willy's voice finally floated to me.

"Stop? I *told* you. Even after I died, I couldn't

stop. I love it so much. Thanks for being my partner, Jeffrey. Now I don't have to stop. I don't ever have to stop . . . not ever!"

"Noooo!" I shouted. "Please! My fingers hurt! I have to stop! I have to! PLEASE!"

"Jeffrey!" My bedroom door flew open. The light clicked on. Dad stood in the doorway.

"Dad! I'm sorry," I cried. "Please help me. Help me!"

Huh?

Dad's face broke into a big smile. "That sounds great, Jeffrey! How did you learn to play like that? Wait till your mom hears. That's excellent! Keep playing! Keep playing!"

TUNE IN TOMORROW

"See you tomorrow!" Elizabeth called over her shoulder.

Lauren nodded. "Same old time. Same old place. Same old . . . stuff!"

Elizabeth laughed. She and Lauren always said good-bye that way. *Of course* they would see each other tomorrow. They were best friends!

Elizabeth hopped on her silver twelve-speed bike and sped home. Every now and then she waved to a neighbor.

Everyone knew everyone in Westgate.

Westgate. The typical American town.

Dinner was already on the table when Elizabeth got home. No surprise there. Dinner was always on the table at six o'clock sharp at the Stephens's house.

"Sorry, Mom," Elizabeth said as she raced in through the front door. "I was with Lauren. I just spaced on the time."

"I don't know what you two girls talk about all day," Elizabeth's father grumbled.

"*Boys*, is my guess," her mother teased. "What else do twelve-year-old girls talk about?"

"Oh, Mother, puh-leeze," Elizabeth groaned as she sat down at the table. She poked at her meat loaf and spinach.

Baron, the family beagle, padded over and rested his paw on her chair. As soon as Mrs. Stephens looked away, Elizabeth sneaked the dog a clump of her spinach. Baron growled. He wanted the meat loaf.

Elizabeth hadn't always lived in Westgate. Up until six months ago, she lived in Philadelphia. Then her dad took a job as Chief of Police of Westgate.

Elizabeth had to leave her friends behind. She even had to say good-bye to Lucky, the hamster she shared with her friend Mary. Mrs. Stephens said she didn't want any rodents in the new house.

It was raining when Elizabeth awoke the next morning. She slipped into a pair of shorts and a T-shirt. Then she plodded her way downstairs.

"Good morning, dear." Mrs. Stephens placed a tray of scrambled eggs and sausage on the table. "I guess you won't be meeting Lauren today. The weather report says we're in for a major tropical storm. They are warning everyone to stay inside."

"Did Dad go to work today?" Elizabeth asked between bites.

"Of course." Her mother sighed. "The Chief of Police can't stay home because of a storm."

The phone rang. "I'll get it," Elizabeth said. She jumped up and grabbed the cordless phone.

"Hey, Lauren!" Elizabeth said into the receiver. "Yeah. I know. My mother just told me the same thing. Oh, well. I'll call you tomorrow."

Elizabeth hung up the phone and scowled. "*Now* what am I supposed to do? This place is so boring!"

Elizabeth's mother frowned. "Maybe it would make you feel better if you wrote a letter to a friend back in Philadelphia."

"And tell her what? That the grass grows really slowly here?"

Mrs. Stephens shrugged. "I'm sure you'll think of something to write," she said.

Elizabeth trudged into the living room. She flopped onto the couch and picked up the remote. "Nothing else to do but watch TV," she told Baron.

In Philadelphia, Elizabeth's parents didn't get cable. They said it was a waste of money. But here they had no choice. You needed cable to get any channels at all. Cable was really cool. Seventy-two different channels!

Elizabeth channel-surfed for a while. She didn't see anything interesting . . . until she reached channel six.

"Coming up next, on *Looking Toward Tomorrow*, twelve-year-old Elinor hears from someone she left behind," the TV announcer said.

"Hey! I never heard of this show before," Elizabeth muttered. "A new soap. Not a bad way to spend an afternoon."

Elizabeth settled back and watched the TV. A blond girl appeared on the screen and flopped into a green velvet chair.

"Another boring day in this dumb old town," the TV character said. She swung her long blond ponytail over her shoulder. "Nothing ever happens here!"

"Boy, can I relate," Elizabeth agreed. She flipped *her* long blond ponytail over *her* shoulder.

The girl on the screen was Elinor. Elizabeth liked her immediately.

Elizabeth watched as Elinor got up off her couch and went into the kitchen to pour herself some fruit punch. Elinor kept looking at the clock. She was waiting for something. But what?

Elinor's fruit punch made Elizabeth thirsty. She went into the kitchen and poured herself a glass of juice. Then she went back to watch the action on *Looking Toward Tomorrow*.

On the show, a loud bell rang. The sound of a grandfather clock. It startled Elinor. She dropped her glass. Slivers of blue and white crystal shattered all over the room. But, somehow, Elinor wasn't hurt.

Elizabeth gasped as something warm and hairy brushed against her bare leg. "YIKES!" she cried. The glass slid from her grip.

CRASH! The crystal shattered on the floor.

Baron scooted out from beneath the couch.

"Dumb dog!" Elizabeth scolded. "You scared me!" She bent down and gingerly picked up a piece of broken glass.

Elizabeth turned back to the TV. Elinor's doorbell rang. The actress stood and opened the door. Elinor found herself face-to-face with a strange-looking man. His beady eyes peered through the glass storm door. His twisted smile seemed dangerous. Still, Elinor opened the door.

"I'm your new neighbor, Elinor," the man on the TV said, introducing himself. He handed Elinor a pink envelope. "This letter came to my house instead of yours. Hope it's good news."

"Fat chance," Elizabeth snickered. "Everyone knows letters *never* bring good news on soap operas!"

Elizabeth was startled by the ring of her own doorbell. She strode to the door and peeked through the window. A small man in a black trench coat stared back at her. He smiled through the glass.

"Hey, there. I'm your new neighbor, Joe Trent," the man shouted through the glass. "This letter came to my house instead of yours." The man held up a small purple envelope.

Elinor opened the door a crack and took the letter from his hand.

"Hope it's good news," Mr. Trent said as he walked away from the door.

"Wow! That's weird," Elizabeth muttered to herself. "That's the same thing that neighbor on TV said."

Elizabeth took the letter back to the couch. Elinor was already reading *her* letter. "Oh, no!" Elinor exclaimed. "This is terrible!"

"What? What does it say?" Elizabeth called to the TV. But the show was over.

Oh, well. Elizabeth still had her *own* letter to read. She glanced at the return address. Awesome! A letter from Mary back in Philadelphia.

Elizabeth's eyes shifted to the TV. This was getting kind of scary. Everything that happened to Elinor was happening to Elizabeth too. The breaking glass. The letter from the stranger. What if there was bad news in this letter too?

"You're nuts!" Elizabeth told herself. It's just a coincidence. She tore open the envelope and pulled out the sheet of purple paper.

DEAR LIZ, the letter began, SUMMER HERE IS PRETTY MUCH THE SAME AS ALWAYS. I WENT TO THE ART MUSEUM YESTERDAY AND WATCHED THE TOURISTS RUN UP AND DOWN THE STEPS LIKE ROCKY IN THE MOVIES. BOY, DID THEY LOOK STUPID!

Elizabeth giggled.

LIZ, the letter continued, I KNOW I PROMISED I

18

WOULD VISIT YOU THIS SUMMER, BUT KATHY MOR-
RISON ASKED ME TO GO TO HER PLACE AT THE JER-
SEY SHORE. I HOPE YOU UNDERSTAND.

P.S. LUCKY ESCAPED FROM HIS CAGE LAST WEEK.
WE LOOKED ALL OVER, BUT WE DIDN'T FIND HIM
UNTIL IT WAS TOO LATE. I BURIED HIM IN THE YARD.
SORRY.

Elizabeth crunched the letter into a tight ball
and shot it into the trash.

The rain and wind were still raging outside
when Elizabeth awoke the next day. But Elizabeth didn't mind. It was the perfect excuse for
watching another episode of *Looking Toward Tomorrow*.

The morning passed really slowly. Elizabeth
watched the clock all morning long. It seemed
like forever until one o'clock — until *Looking Toward Tomorrow*.

Finally, Elizabeth plopped down on the couch,
picked up the remote, and flicked on channel six.

Elizabeth's mother came out of the kitchen.
"What are you doing?" she asked.

"Watching TV. Something called *Looking Toward Tomorrow*," Elizabeth replied.

"Oh, Elizabeth! Not one of those silly soap operas." Mrs. Stephens sighed. "Those shows are all
about things that could never happen," she said.

"That's not true," Elizabeth insisted. "This
show is very realistic!"

19

She squinted at the TV as the story started. Elinor was still sitting on her couch, exactly where she was the day before. She was still reading her letter unhappily.

Elizabeth moved to the edge of *her* couch. She couldn't wait to find out what Elinor's letter said.

BANG! THUD!

Elinor jumped from her perch on the couch. So did Elizabeth. The offstage noise scared both of them.

"Mother! Mother! Are you all right?" Elinor cried.

There was no reply.

Elinor raced down the stairs to the basement. The show went to a commercial.

Elizabeth's heart was still pounding when *Looking Toward Tomorrow* returned. By this time, Elinor had made her way down to the dark basement. Soot and steam hung in the air.

"The boiler must have exploded!" Elinor exclaimed. "Mom! Mom! Where are you?"

Suddenly, the camera focused on an older woman. She was lying silently on the floor. Thick pieces of broken wood and metal covered her.

"Mother! Mother! Speak to me!" Elinor cried out.

The mother's eyes fluttered open. "Where am I?" she asked Elinor. "Do I know you?"

The screen faded to black.

Elizabeth laughed out loud. Only on TV, she thought as she clicked off the TV set.

Suddenly the ceiling rumbled over Elizabeth's head. She heard a heavy *THUD*.

"Mom! Mom! Are you all right?" Elizabeth shrieked.

There was no reply.

Elizabeth raced up the stairs to her parents' bedroom.

Outside, the raging winds had knocked down an old tree. It had crashed through the upstairs window!

Elizabeth lowered her eyes to the floor. "Oh, no!" she cried.

Elizabeth's mother was lying on the floor. A huge tree limb had fallen over her. Pieces of wood and glass covered her.

Elizabeth frantically grabbed the phone and dialed 9-1-1. "Send an ambulance to 60 Fernwood Way," she said. "And hurry."

She hung up. Then she called her father. Then she waited with her mother until the ambulance came.

"Don't worry, Mom," Elizabeth said as the emergency crew carried her mother out on a stretcher. "Daddy is going to meet us at the hospital."

Mrs. Stephens's eyes fluttered open. "Where am I?" she asked Elizabeth. "Do I know you?"

21

Elizabeth had a sick feeling in the pit of her stomach.

This can't be happening, she told herself. Her heart pounded in her chest. I just saw this whole scene happen to Elinor on TV.

"Daddy, I'm so glad you're here!" Elizabeth exclaimed when her father joined her in the emergency waiting room. "I'm so worried about Mom. There's something really strange going on. I've been watching this TV show, and —"

A nurse interrupted. "Excuse me, Chief Stephens. You may see your wife now," she said.

The chief smiled bravely at Elizabeth. "Honey, why don't you go stay at Lauren's for a while?" he suggested. "I don't want you to be alone."

Elizabeth nodded. She didn't *want* to be alone. Too many scary things were happening lately.

Elizabeth left the hospital and raced to Lauren's house. She arrived soaked and worried and frightened.

"Elizabeth! What are you doing here?" Lauren asked as she opened the door.

"Lauren, something weird is happening," Elizabeth said. "I've been watching the soap opera *Looking Toward Tomorrow.* You know it?"

Lauren shook her head. "Never heard of it."

"It's about a girl named Elinor. She's twelve, and she hates living in a small town."

"Sounds good," Lauren said. "But it doesn't sound weird."

"I haven't gotten to the weird part yet," Elizabeth explained. "The weird part started yesterday. First Elinor dropped a glass. Then I dropped a glass. Then a weird neighbor brought Elinor a letter with bad news. Then some guy I've never seen brings *me* a letter with bad news."

Lauren laughed. "Big deal. Those things could happen to anyone."

"That's what I thought," Elizabeth replied. "Until today. On today's show, Elinor's mom got hit in the head. And she lost her memory."

"Only on TV," Lauren snickered.

"I thought so too," Elizabeth replied. "But then a huge tree smashed into our house and whacked *my* mom on the head. She's at the hospital right now. And she doesn't remember who I am!"

Lauren put her arm around Elizabeth. "Hey. Your mom will be okay," she assured her.

"I guess," Elizabeth replied shakily. "But I won't really know how she'll be until one o'clock tomorrow."

"Is that when her test results come back?" Lauren asked.

"No. That's when the show comes on," Elizabeth said. "That's when I'll find out how *Elinor's* mother is doing."

Lauren stared at Elizabeth. "You are really losing it!" she scolded.

"No. I'm serious," Elizabeth said in a whisper.

Lauren changed the subject. "You want to go shopping with me tomorrow afternoon? Only three more weeks till school starts!"

Elizabeth stared at her friend. Hadn't Lauren been listening? "I can't go shopping!" she insisted. "I have to watch *Looking Toward Tomorrow.*"

"You're just upset about your mom," Lauren said. "But she'll be fine. I'm sure she will."

The next day, at five minutes to one, Elizabeth's father called from the hospital. "Elizabeth, are you coming here?" he asked. "Visiting hours begin at one."

Elizabeth wanted to go see her mother. But she couldn't. She couldn't risk missing *Looking Toward Tomorrow.*

"I'll try to get there by two," Elizabeth told her dad. "There's something I need to do first."

"All right," Elizabeth's dad replied. "I'll call if there's any change."

Elizabeth's hand shook as she hung up the phone. No matter what, she would not — *could not* — miss that show. She had to find out what was going to happen to Elinor's mother . . . and to Elinor!

Elizabeth turned on the TV. As the show

started, Elinor was at home. She paced the floor, waiting for a call from the hospital.

Suddenly Elinor was startled by a dog barking off-camera.

Baron barked back at the TV set.

"It seems so *real*, doesn't it, Baron?" Elizabeth whispered, hugging the beagle.

Elizabeth watched as Elinor walked slowly toward the door. Elinor laced her fingers around the doorknob and opened the door.

"Oh, no!" Elizabeth cried out. She watched as Elinor came face-to-face with a vicious, barking rottweiler! The dog bared its long fangs. With an angry howl, it leaped at Elinor. Then . . .

The TV screen went blank.

"No! NO! NO!" Elizabeth screamed. She clicked the remote frantically. The screen stayed black. Elizabeth banged furiously on the top of the TV set.

No picture. No sound.

What had happened? A blown fuse? The TV set broke?

Elizabeth *had* to know what happened to Elinor's mother. And to Elinor! Her hand trembled as she picked up the phone and called Lauren.

"Hello! Lauren!" she cried. "Have you been watching *Looking Toward Tomorrow*?"

"I tried to," Lauren replied. "But when I turned to channel six, all I got was static."

Elizabeth hung up quickly. She grabbed the

25

phone book. Maybe she could call channel six and find out what happened on the show.

"Huh?"

Channel six wasn't listed in the phone book.

But the phone number of the cable company was there. Elizabeth quickly dialed the number. Maybe someone there could give her the phone number for channel six.

"Hello. Westgate Cable," the cable operator said. "How may I help you?"

"Can you give me the phone number for channel six?" Elizabeth demanded.

Through the receiver she could hear computer keys clicking. Then the operator spoke. "There is no channel six on your cable system," she said.

"Excuse me? That's impossible," Elizabeth insisted. "I've been watching *Looking Toward Tomorrow* on channel six all week long."

"I'm sorry. We don't have a channel six," the woman repeated.

Elizabeth's hands shook as she hung up the phone.

She heard a lot of noise outside. Baron began barking fiercely. He raced to the front door.

Feeling dazed, Elizabeth glided toward the door. She wrapped her fingers around the knob, and . . .

"Don't do it!" I shouted at the TV.

My friend Lisa clicked off the set. "Doesn't she

26

get it?" Lisa asked. "It's going to be a vicious rottweiler at the front door."

Lisa sighed. "I thought *Life with Elizabeth* was going to be really good. But it's just another stupid soap opera."

"Yeah," I agreed. "Why are people on TV so dumb?"

LIVE BAIT

There's one thing you should know before I tell you this story: I HATE fish.

I hate their cold, clammy, scaly skin. I hate their slimy, slippery fins. And I hate their flat, glassy fish eyes!

That's why I hate summer vacations at Lake Bigelow. There are fish *everywhere* — at the docks, at the market, in the restaurants. Even the road signs have pictures of fish on them!

Worst of all, Dad catches fish *every day*. Mom cooks fish *every day*. And I'm expected to EAT fish *every day*.

Yuck.

"You're *afraid* of fish, aren't you, Timmy?" Duke teased me one afternoon.

I don't like Duke. He's a mean kid. But there is no one else to hang out with at the beach.

"I am *not* afraid of fish," I protested. "I just don't *like* them."

Duke poked me in the ribs. Hard. "If you're not afraid — prove it!"

I rubbed my ribs. "How?" I asked.

"Let's go fishing," he suggested. "Out on the lake. We'll rent a boat!"

"Fishing? In a boat?" I gulped. "I don't think my parents will let me."

"Are you *scared*?" Duke snickered.

"No! N-no way!" I sputtered. "I . . . I just don't have money to rent a boat."

"Don't worry," Duke scoffed. "I've got plenty of money." He patted his jeans pocket and grabbed my arm. "Let's go, Tim Boy!"

Duke was big and stubborn, so I couldn't back down. I had to prove to him that I wasn't scared. I followed him down the road to the fishing docks.

The smell was terrible. *Fish* smell. So . . . fishy.

Buckets of fresh fish lined the wooden walkway around the lake. I tiptoed carefully around the buckets.

Something tickled my neck.

Something *slimy*!

I cried out — and spun around.

Duke shoved a big dead trout into my face. "Hungry, Timmy?" he leered.

I jumped back and watched in disgust as Duke *plucked out one of the fish's eyes*. "Oh, noooo," I moaned.

The fish eye was round and gooey. Duke rolled it between his fingers, then thrust it toward me. "Take a look!"

I staggered backwards.

Duke giggled.

And popped the fish eye into his mouth!

"YUCK!" My stomach heaved. I nearly lost my lunch.

Duke spit out the eye. Then he held the dead fish in front of me. "Here's another juicy eyeball for you," he chuckled. "Have a taste!"

I panicked. I pulled away — and tripped over a bucket of trout. The slimy fish spilled across the dock. I tumbled on top of them.

"GROSS!"

A sticky fish fin slapped me across the face! I yelped and scrambled to my feet.

Duke howled with laughter. "Tim Boy, you *are* afraid! Afraid of fish!"

"I am *not* afraid!" I shouted. "I just don't like fish!"

Duke grinned. "So you're going fishing with me?"

What choice did I have? "Okay," I agreed. "As long as I don't have to eat any fish eyes."

Duke grinned and tugged my arm. "Come on!" he ordered. "Let's find a boat before they're all rented!"

He dragged me from pier to pier. "Do you have

a boat to rent?" he shouted to the fishermen. The answer was no. All the boats were taken.

I breathed a sigh of relief. *No boat, no fishing.* I was saved.

"Look!" Duke cried. "There's one more pier, down there at the end of the dock."

He pointed to a rickety dock in the distance.

My heart sank in my chest. It was the *creepiest* pier I had ever seen. It stood alone at the edge of the lake, where the trees grew tall and thick. It sagged and dipped across the water. It looked as if it might sink into the lake at any moment.

"You've got to be kidding," I muttered.

"No! Come on!" Duke urged. "It's our last chance to go fishing!"

Duke pushed me toward the pier. I stumbled ahead into the shadows of the woods. The birds and crickets must have heard us, because they stopped chirping.

The silence made me shiver.

"This is crazy," I protested. "There are no boats out here."

Duke pointed at the end of the pier. "See that little shack?" he asked. "It says 'Live Bait' on the side."

"That sign must be a hundred years old!" I argued.

Duke shook his head. "You really are afraid,

aren't you?" He smirked. "What a baby! Afraid of a few little fish!"

I could feel my face turn red. "I am NOT a baby!" I snapped back. "And I'll prove it." I clenched my fists and stomped onto the pier.

The boards creaked beneath my feet.

"Come on, Duke," I growled. "I'll prove that I'm *not* afraid of those stupid fish! In fact, I'm going to catch the *biggest* fish of all!"

"All right!" Duke cheered. "A fishing contest!"

He darted past me and charged down the pier. I moved forward carefully. The rotting old boards cracked and crunched. The whole pier swayed with my weight. I felt seasick!

I stumbled ahead. A wooden plank snapped beneath my feet.

My legs crashed through the pier.

I dropped through.

"DUKE! HELP!" I screamed.

I clung to the pier with both hands. My feet kicked and splashed in the icy lake. "DUU-UUKE!"

Duke scampered down the pier as fast as he could. The pier rocked from side to side. "Hold on, Timmy!" he shouted. "I'm here! Reach for my hand!"

I stretched out my arm and grasped his hand. Duke pulled with a grunt. The boards cracked beneath my chest as I pulled myself up. I swung my leg onto a plank.

The plank broke.

"DUUUKE!" I screamed as I fell.

I held on with one hand and dangled beneath the pier. My legs plunged once again into the cold water.

"Ohhhhh." I moaned as something nipped at my ankles. "Hurry, Duke!" I wailed. "The fish are trying to eat me!"

Duke grabbed my wrist and pulled as hard as he could. Slowly I flopped up onto the pier, gasping for breath.

Duke burst out laughing. *"The fish are trying to eat me!"* he mocked. "You are such a baby!"

I didn't answer him. I stood up and marched toward the end of the pier. I stomped up to the little fishing shack. I lifted my hand to pound on the door, but I stopped.

I didn't like the looks of this place.

Duke crept up behind me and pushed me forward. "Go ahead," he dared. "Knock on the door."

I clenched my fist and knocked.

Something crashed inside the shack. Duke and I jumped back.

The door swung open.

We gazed down at a broken jar in the doorway. Dozens of slimy green worms oozed at our feet.

"Gross!" I cried.

A voice rang out from the darkness of the shack. "You wouldn't think so if you were a fish!"

Duke and I raised our heads and peered inside. A friendly-looking old man with a white beard stepped forward. "Do you boys want to buy some bait?" he asked.

Duke and I smiled. "Yes, sir! We're going to catch some HUGE fish!" Duke bragged.

The old man chuckled. "You've come to the right place, boys," he said with a tug of his beard. "Step inside, step inside."

Duke strode in, and I followed. I tiptoed carefully over the slimy green worms in the doorway.

The door slammed behind me.

My heart jumped. I stared into the darkness. And I couldn't believe my eyes.

Hundreds and hundreds of glass jars filled the room. Some jars were big. Some were small. And some bubbled and glowed as if they were some sort of laboratory experiment.

The jars were filled with all sorts of icky little creatures. Brown worms, black worms, red worms, centipedes, millipedes, bluebottle flies, greenbottle flies, and shiny round fish eggs of all sizes and colors.

"What's in this one?" I asked. I pressed my finger against a jar full of cloudy water.

A silver baby eel snapped at the glass.

I snatched my finger back.

Duke and the old man laughed at me.

"I've never seen so many kinds of fishing bait,"

Duke gushed. "You must be an awesome fisher-man."

The old man grinned. His teeth gleamed in the dim light. "You might say I'm an expert on bait," he replied. "I've been fishing my whole life. And I like to experiment with my bait. You see, some fish only like red worms. Other fish only like spi-ders. And certain fish are so picky, they will only eat a five-course dinner with a glass of wine!"

Duke laughed at the joke, but I didn't think it was very funny.

"So how can I help you boys?" the old man asked. "Let me guess. You need some bait, some fishing poles, and a boat. Am I right?"

Duke nodded. "Ah . . . how much . . . for an hour?" he stammered.

The old man squinted. "For you two boys? Let's see. How about seven dollars an hour."

Duke reached into his pocket and pulled out a crumpled five-dollar bill. "This is all I have," he said.

The old man rubbed his whiskers. "Hmmm. I'll make a deal with you," he said. "If you give me the biggest fish you catch, I won't charge you a penny. Is it a deal?"

"Deal!" Duke replied.

"Deal!" I repeated.

The old man winked and nodded.

My heart sank when I saw the boat. It was

rickety and old, and covered with green moss and slime. The oars jutted out like two skinny toothpicks. And it rocked wildly back and forth when we tried to climb aboard.

I stumbled and pitched forward. I almost fell over the side!

"Careful," warned the old fisherman. "Don't fall in the water . . . unless you can swim like a fish!"

I thought about all those big ugly fish in the lake. I shivered. "Don't worry," I mumbled. "I'm staying right here in this boat."

Duke shook his head. "Timmy is afraid of fish," he said, chuckling.

"I am not!" I cried. "Come on! Let's go fishing!"

The old fisherman handed us two fishing poles and a jar of worms. "Good luck, boys," he hooted. "Hope you catch a real whopper!"

He gently pushed the boat away from the dock. Duke rowed. I nervously whistled "Row, Row, Row Your Boat" as we glided toward the middle of the lake.

I already felt seasick!

Duke stopped rowing. "Here, take a worm," he ordered. "Stick it on your hook like this."

I shuddered as Duke slipped a fat brown worm onto the hook of his fishing line. I sighed and reached into the jar for another one.

"Yuck," I groaned. The worm was so sticky, it

left a trail of goo across my fingers. I hate worms almost as much as I hate fish.

I took a deep breath and stuck the wriggling creature onto my hook.

Duke showed me how to cast my fishing line into the water. I swung the rod over my head. The worm plopped into the water ten feet away from the boat. "Is that okay?" I asked Duke.

"Fine," he answered.

I gazed out at the water. I heard a splash in the distance. A fish. I jumped.

And almost tipped the boat over!

"Just sit there quietly and wait," Duke ordered.

So we sat there quietly. And waited. And waited.

And waited for a long, long time.

"I think that old man sold us bad bait," Duke complained.

"I'm bored," I said, moaning. "Let's go back. There are no fish out here. That old man doesn't know anything about — FIIIISSSHHH!"

I shrieked in horror.

As the biggest fish in the world rose up from the lake!

Its enormous silvery head was bigger than a truck. Its giant bulging fish eyes rolled in their sockets. Its immense fins churned high, crashing waves in the water.

The waves tossed our tiny boat up and down. I screamed and grabbed Duke. "It's heading right for us!"

Duke screeched in terror and handed me an oar. *"Hit it!"* he cried.

The huge sea monster vanished below the surface of the lake. For a moment, everything was calm. I clutched the oar and waited.

Duke wailed. "TIMMY!"

I spun around.

And stared into the colossal jaws of the monster fish!

"AAAAIIIII!" Duke and I both swung our oars at its ferocious head.

The sea beast plunged down. A snap of its jaws crushed our oars.

"HOLD ON!" Duke screamed.

The boat pitched forward.

Into the fish's mouth!

"NOOOOOOOO!" I opened my mouth in an endless scream. Oozing gobs of fish goo slithered against my skin. The fish's mouth slammed shut, and the boat plunged down . . . down . . .

Into the fish's belly!

"Timmy! We — we're trapped!" Duke gasped.

My voice echoed in the vast, dark belly as I shrieked, "WE'RE FISH FOOD!"

In the darkness, I saw hundreds of fish floating all around us. A tide of fish flopped into the boat.

They wriggled and slapped against us. One little fish tried to wriggle into my mouth!

I spat it out and screamed, "GET ME OUT OF HERE! DUKE!"

Duke couldn't help me. He was too busy screaming too.

The fish stomach churned faster. The water gushed and sprayed. The fish flipped and flopped in and out of our boat.

"Duke! What's happening?" I screeched.

"Hold on to the boat!" he cried.

I clung tightly to the sides. The tiny rowboat lurched backwards.

Duke and I screamed.

The boat rocked. Then it plunged toward the fish's mouth . . .

And *freedom*!

The jaws popped open. Our boat fell and crashed. We flew out — and landed hard.

"We're free!" I cheered. Then I gasped. "Hey — where are we?"

It took me a while to recognize the wooden planks of the old pier. The sun blazed in the sky. I squinted my eyes, gazed up . . .

And saw the old man from the bait shop.

He grinned. "Congratulations, boys!" he whooped. "You've made an old man very happy. You brought me the catch of the century!"

Duke and I scrambled to our feet. We wiped

the slime and water from our faces. Then we turned around.

The monstrous fish lay lifeless across the pier. It was bigger than a house! Its fishy belly glistened in the sunlight. Its fish eyes — as big as basketballs — stared blankly.

The old man cackled and danced. "I've been trying to catch Old Jumbo for fifty years!" he exclaimed. "You boys were *just the bait I needed!*"

"Huh?" Duke choked out.

"B-bait?" I stammered. *"Us?"*

The old man stepped aside to reveal a giant glass jar.

Before we could move, he threw a net over our heads. Then he hoisted us into the jar.

As I dropped to the bottom of the jar, I glimpsed the label on the side. It read:

LIVE BAIT

SOMETHING STRANGE
ABOUT MARCI

We all knew from the beginning that there was something strange about Marci.

One day she just appeared.

We didn't see her move in. We never saw her family.

One day, there she was. She stood behind the bushes, staring at us across the park.

She didn't move. She didn't speak.

Did she think we didn't see her? Was she trying to hide from us?

At first, my friends and I ignored her. She seemed so unfriendly. So cold.

Why didn't she walk right up to us? Why didn't she greet us and introduce herself?

My friends and I were playing some kind of crazy game. We were running around a tree, tagging each other, then rolling to safety.

It felt so good to be outdoors. It had been a cold, rainy spring. Rainwater still glistened on the tree leaves and the tall grass. I liked the way it made my bare feet tingle when I ran.

We played our game and didn't pay any attention to Marci.

Of course, we didn't know her name yet. We didn't learn her name until much later. And by the time we learned it, we already knew there was something strange about her.

Something scary.

I admit it. I glanced back at her as we played our silly game. I watched her standing so still, staring back at me. And that cold, cold expression on her face — it frightened me. It really did.

What did she plan to do?

Did she plan to stand there all afternoon without coming over to us? Without making a sound?

Why was she staring at us like that? I could practically feel her bright blue eyes burning into me.

Where did she come from? Where was the rest of her family?

I had so many questions for her. So many things I wanted to know. Normal things when someone new moves into your neighborhood.

But I couldn't ask her anything if she stayed frozen behind the bushes.

The game went on behind me. One of my friends began laughing at the top of her lungs. She was positively *screeching*.

You know how it is. When someone starts

laughing, pretty soon everyone is laughing. You can't help it. It's contagious, I guess.

So we all started laughing. For no reason at all. Just because we felt like being silly.

Pretty soon, we were slapping each other high fives. Rolling around in the grass, and just acting rowdy.

It was spring, after all.

When I finally got myself together, I glanced back at the bushes. And Marci was gone.

I felt a chill.

Did we frighten her away?

We were only having fun. Why was she so unfriendly?

The next few days were rainy. The new spring leaves trembled in the gusting winds.

We didn't see Marci. I thought about her a few times. I thought about her cold stare. About the way she stood so stiffly behind the bushes.

On the afternoon after the rain stopped, my friends and I hiked up a hill and had a picnic. I was so hungry. I had slept right through breakfast.

My friends laughed at me because of the way I gobbled down my food. One of them playfully tried to push me down the hill. I shoved her away.

That's when I saw Marci. She was standing at the bottom of the hill. She had one hand raised, shielding her eyes from the bright sunlight.

I poked my friend and pointed down the hill. We all saw her. We all froze.

Was she going to climb up and join us?

She didn't move.

So I took the first step. I'm a friendly guy. I don't like to see someone standing outside the crowd.

I waved to her. I motioned for her to join us.

Some of my friends waved too. And we called to her.

Marci took a few steps and then stopped.

My friends and I exchanged confused glances. What was her *problem*?

We were inviting her to join our picnic. Why was she being so unfriendly?

I think that's when the idea struck me. Just a tiny idea at the back of my mind. A tiny, frightening idea that refused to go away.

Marci is evil.

The idea crept into my thoughts and stuck there.

Marci is evil.

Of course I had no proof. I guess you could call it a hunch. But the way she stared up at us, ignoring our calls and our waves — well, it gave me a chill.

Even on such a warm, beautiful spring day, it gave me a chill.

The next time I saw Marci, I was all alone.

I had been walking all over the neighborhood,

searching for my friends. But I couldn't find any of them at home.

Maybe they're hanging out at the lake, I decided. It was a cloudy day, still too cold to swim. But my friends and I liked to meet at the lake and just mess around.

I was half-walking, half-jogging along the path to the shore when I suddenly had the feeling I was being followed.

Yes!

The snap of a twig gave her away. And then I heard her cough.

I spun around and saw Marci far down the dirt path. She was walking rapidly, swinging her arms as she walked. But when I turned, she stopped.

My heart pounded. I was startled to see her.

I felt a little afraid without my friends. She was so strange, I didn't really like being all alone with her.

What did she want? Was she following me?

Once again, she froze and didn't come any closer.

I stared at her, scratching my forehead. I couldn't decide what to do. Should I run? Was I in danger?

Or should I walk up to her and greet her?

Yes, I decided. Enough of this awkwardness. Enough of this suspense. I'll go over to her and make her feel welcome.

I took a few steps and then stopped.

Marci had a square black case strapped over her shoulder. As I started to come near to her, she swung the case around and began to open it.

I froze. Panic swept down my body.

Marci is evil.

The thought returned.

She started to pull something from the case. Something black. It glinted in the light.

I didn't wait to find out what it was.

I took a deep breath and bolted off the path and into the trees.

I tried to convince my friends that Marci was evil. They didn't want to listen to me. They just wanted to goof around and be rowdy.

So *what* if she's strange? So *what* if she doesn't want to be our friend?

That was *their* attitude.

But I couldn't stop thinking about her. About the case strapped to her shoulder. About my frightening feeling that she meant us harm.

I decided to take action. I decided to find out more about Marci. The next time I see her, I decided, I'm going to follow her home.

I didn't have to wait long.

The next day, I spotted her as I made my way to my friend's place. I was following the dirt path that led to the lake. She stood off the path, half-hidden by tall weeds.

I gasped when I saw the case hanging from her shoulder.

But I took a deep breath and decided to be brave. I called out to her. I waved. I flashed her my friendliest smile.

She stared back at me blankly. She didn't smile or wave back.

Was she pretending that she didn't hear me? That she didn't see me?

I felt so hurt. Why did she have to be so unfriendly?

Once again, she reached for the case. So once again I darted into the woods.

This time I didn't run away. I hid behind a pile of rocks. I could see Marci on the path. She was searching for me.

Why? I wondered. What did she plan to do to me?

She gave up the search after a few minutes. I saw her turn back and start to walk away. Creeping as silently as I could over the wet grass and leaves, I followed her.

I felt excited and terrified at the same time.

What would she do if she caught me sneaking after her? Where was she going?

After a while, she stepped off the path and pushed her way through clumps of bushes and tangled weeds. I stayed pretty far behind. A couple of times, I almost lost her.

The sun came out and made my back tingle and

itch. I stopped at the edge of a round, grassy clearing. Hiding behind a tree, I watched Marci go into her home.

A tent!

I stared in disbelief. I forced myself to creep up closer. Close enough to see through the narrow opening of the tent flap.

Marci had no family, I saw. No family at all.

She lived all alone. And she lived in a tent!

Why? I wondered. Why is Marci so totally strange?

The mystery wasn't cleared up until the next afternoon.

My friends and I were goofing off as usual. It was a sunny, sparkling day. Almost as warm as summer.

A couple of my friends wanted to go fishing in the lake. I wasn't in the mood. I was hungry. I wanted to get something to eat.

We couldn't decide what to do. So we didn't do much of anything at all.

Imagine our surprise when Marci came stepping out of the woods.

She stopped a few feet away from us. And smiled for the first time.

I didn't like that smile. I admit it. It scared me.

She had never smiled at us before. Why was she smiling now?

I took a step back. My friends were all studying her, waiting to see what she had in mind.

I saw the case strapped on her shoulder. And I saw a brown paper bag in her hands.

She took a step closer to us. Closer.

"Hello!" she called. "Hello!"

My heart nearly stopped.

She reached into the bag. She pulled out something — and held it out to me!

Food!

She pulled more from the bag. She had brought us food!

Was she finally trying to be friendly?

Should I be friendly too? I wondered. Should I walk up to her? Should I help myself to some food?

My stomach growled. I was so hungry.

I held my breath and took a small step. Then another. Then I took a piece of fruit from her hand.

As soon as I grabbed the fruit, Marci swung the case around.

I jumped back.

She reached into the case — and pulled out something black and slender, attached to a cord.

I gasped as she raised the object to her mouth. She spoke into it. "Testing . . . testing . . ." she said.

My friends and I all cast curious glances at one another. What on earth was going on here?

"This is Dr. Marci Gould," Marci spoke into the slender object. "I have been observing the subjects for nine days. Today, on day ten, I made personal contact with them."

And that's when the mystery was cleared up.

That's when I realized why Marci was so strange. That's when I realized why Marci was so different from us.

That's when I realized that Marci wasn't an orangutan.

THE GHOST SITTER

Ray was worried.

He and his family had recently moved into a funny old house with two staircases and a crooked chimney. Mom and Dad loved to buy old houses and fix them up. But they promised this time would be the last.

"This is our home forever," Mom said. "Crooked chimney and all."

"Beat you to the top!" Mike, Ray's older brother, shouted from the stairway across the hall. He was already halfway up the staircase.

"Meet you in the lookout room!" Ray shouted back. He loved all the funny little rooms in the old house. And he knew the place would look great once his parents finished fixing it up.

That wasn't what worried him.

He was worried about what had happened at recess.

"This town has got its very own haunted house," a skinny kid named Chris told him on the

51

playground. "A run-down old place. When my dog gets anywhere near it, he just sits down and howls."

"And what about the smell?" another kid chimed in. "The house smells like garbage that's been left out for weeks."

Ray shivered. Mike stood next to him on the playground. Mike was smiling. Ray could tell that his brother didn't believe any of it.

"Where is this so-called haunted house?" Mike asked.

"On Beech Street," a girl with braces said.

"The dead end of Beech," Chris added.

"Huh?" Ray uttered. He and Mike lived on Beech Street. At the dead end!

The bell rang, and everyone wandered back into school. Ray walked beside the girl with the braces. "You know that haunted house on Beech Street?" Ray asked.

The girl nodded solemnly.

"Well, is it the one on the right? Or the one on the left?"

"Let's see," the girl said. She thought hard. "Uh . . . the left. Yes. It's the one on the left."

And *that's* what had Ray worried.

The deserted house next door. The one on the left. Ray had already noticed something creepy about it. The lawn was overgrown with weeds. A small window was broken.

It could be haunted. It *looked* haunted.

*   *   *

Mike and Ray walked home after school. "Mike, do you really think the house next door is haunted?" Ray asked.

Mike shook his head. "No way. There's no such thing as a haunted house. Not on our street. Not on anybody's street."

Ray started to feel better. Mike sounded so sure.

He smiled when he saw his mother. She was busy planting bright red geraniums in the window boxes on their front porch. It was really beginning to look like home.

"Hi, Mom," Ray called as he ran up the front path. But then he froze.

Something was wrong. He could feel it.

A chill ran up his back. He had the feeling someone was watching him. He turned to the house next door.

His gaze wandered up to the peeling paint on the side of the house. He spotted a small, round window in the top of the house — *and there they were!*

Two eyes. Dark, angry eyes. Staring down at him.

He gasped.

The eyes vanished.

"Mike," he whispered. "I — I think I just saw the ghost. Up in that window."

Mike glanced up at the empty window. Then he

53

shook his head. "Don't let the kids at school spook you."

"I've got a job for you two," their mother said, dropping her gardening trowel.

Mike groaned. "I've got homework, Mom. Can't Ray do it?"

"It's a job for *both* of you," she said. "You're going to house-sit for the sweet old couple next door while they're away."

Ray's eyes bulged. His mouth dropped open. "You mean somebody actually *lives* there?"

"Mr. and Mrs. Hodge," their mother replied. "I met them today. I think they've lived there forever. You just have to do a few chores for them Saturday morning and again at night."

"At night?" Ray gasped. "Do we have to sleep there?"

His mother laughed. "Of course not. The Hodges will be back Sunday morning."

Mike sighed. "It's the weekend, Mom. I wanted to hang out with my new friends."

"I promised them, Mike. It won't be any big deal," she insisted. "They told me exactly what they need you to do."

Mike shrugged. "Fine. Whatever."

"Whatever," Ray repeated softly, gazing up at the window next door.

The next morning, they walked across the yard to the house next door. Ray picked up the

Hodges' mail and the newspaper. Then he caught up to Mike on their porch.

He slipped the key into the lock, turned the knob, and gave the heavy wooden door a shove. The door creaked as it swung open on rusty hinges.

The house was quiet. So quiet, Ray could hear the hum of the refrigerator in the kitchen.

They stepped into a long hall. Ray followed so closely behind Mike, he scraped the back of one of Mike's shoes.

"Quit it, Ray," Mike warned. "You're scaring yourself."

"What's that horrible smell?" Ray cried. "Yuck. Like rotten eggs." Ray held his nose.

Mike sniffed. "Um, yeah. I smell it." He coughed. "Gross."

Ray followed him into the kitchen. "It's definitely something rotting." He glanced around nervously.

"Check it out! They've got a dumbwaiter," Mike said. "It's one of those little elevators that goes between floors. Cool!"

He started to open it.

"Don't!" Ray cried. "Let's just do our chores and get out of here."

Mike pulled the dumbwaiter door up halfway.

"Ohhhh! It stinks!" Ray moaned. He backed up. "It's like . . . like something *dead*."

Mike grabbed a dish towel and covered his

nose. He reached into the dumbwaiter carefully and grabbed something. "It's just a bowl of old food," Mike muttered. "Open the garbage can."

Holding his breath to keep out the stench, Ray opened the can. Mike tilted the dish. A dry, green blob plopped into the garbage can.

Ray slammed the lid shut. "What was that?" he gasped.

"Oatmeal." Mike fanned the towel around. "Guess the Hodges forgot it was there."

He put the empty bowl back in the dumb-waiter. "Wonder if it works," he said. He pulled a rope. The elevator tray slid up, carrying the bowl. "Cool."

They both watched it disappear.

"Wonder where it ends up," Ray murmured.

"In the attic, probably," Mike answered.

Ray shivered and remembered the dark eyes staring down at him from the round attic window. He shut the dumbwaiter door. Tight. "Let's go," he said.

"Not so fast, Ray." Mike grabbed his elbow. "We have to open the curtains in the living room."

Ray followed closely after Mike. He was nearly to the dark living room when something soft squished under his shoe.

His heart jumped into his throat. "Yuck! I — I stepped on something. An animal!"

Mike rolled his eyes. He bent down and picked up a soft, cloth doll. "You mean this?" He handed it to Ray.

Ray stared at it. "It has no head, Mike. And look at these teeth marks in the doll's arms."

Mike studied it. "Looks like it's been chewed."

"By what?" Ray demanded.

Mike didn't answer. He began to tug the drapes open.

Something crashed on the floor above them.

This time, Ray's heart leaped up to his *mouth*!

A second loud crash was followed by a deep groan.

"Someone is in this house!" Ray cried. He dove for the front door.

He turned and caught the fear on Mike's face. The two of them roared out of the house and slammed the door behind them.

They flopped down on their porch, out of breath, and stared at the house next door. Ray shivered. "What did we hear? Do you think it was a ghost? Should we tell Mom and Dad?"

"We acted dumb," Mike scolded. "There was no need to run away. Old houses are full of strange noises."

Ray knew his brother was right. All old houses made noises.

"Or it could even be some kids playing a joke," Mike suggested. He started into the house.

"Don't bother Mom and Dad with this. It's no big deal."

"Right. No big deal," Ray echoed.

The black clouds seemed to be gathering right over the house next door. Ray and Mike crossed the yard for the second time that day.

Ray shuddered at the sound of thunder.

They opened the door. "It's so dark in here," Ray whispered. "I can't see a thing."

"I'll find the light switch," Mike whispered back. Ray could hear Mike's hand sliding over the wall.

A loud crack of thunder made them both jump.

Ray heard a click. The hall light flashed on. He breathed a sigh of relief as they edged toward the living room.

"You close the drapes," Mike ordered. "I'll turn the kitchen light on."

Ray started to protest. But Mike was already hurrying away.

Ray made his way slowly to the dark living room. He reached his hand around the corner, feeling for the light switch.

His hand brushed something soft.

He gasped and pulled it back.

He stood still for a moment, hardly daring to breathe. Was it just a cobweb?

Slowly, he reached out again. His fingers fumbled on the switch. He clicked the ceiling light on and stared into the room.

"Whooooa!" he uttered.

He tried to back up — but his legs wouldn't cooperate. He stood frozen. And stared in shock around the room.

What a mess!

The whole room had been trashed!

Ray's knees buckled as a shrill moan floated into the room.

"We've got to get out!" Mike cried. He ran out of the kitchen and pushed Ray out the door.

They ran across the yard, slipping, ducking their heads in the pouring rain.

"What was that noise?" Mike asked when they were safe on their own porch.

"I have no idea," Ray said, struggling to catch his breath. "What was that mess? It looked like a bomb hit the place!"

"Same with the kitchen!" Mike replied. "Garbage was thrown everywhere. What a stink!"

"This is no joke. We've got to tell Mom and Dad," Ray said.

They found their father in a chair in the den. Mom was winding a bandage around his arm.

She shook her head. "The cellar door slammed on your father's arm. He's lucky it isn't broken."

"I'm okay," Dad told them. "I'm just glad this is

the last time we'll ever fix up an old house. It's almost as if this old place is out to get me."

Mom laughed. "Me too. I've had it with do-it-yourself. This is home from now on."

"Let's call it a day," Dad said. He followed Mom up the stairs slowly. "Come to bed, kids."

"Be up in a minute, Mom," Mike called after them. Alone in the kitchen, he and Ray gazed out the window. Lightning lit the sky and outlined the house next door.

"We should have told them," Ray said softly.

"Let's just wait until morning," Mike said. He stared out the window. "Oh, no." He groaned.

"What?" Ray said. "What is it?"

"I left the Hodges' keys in their kitchen. And I didn't even lock the door." He shook his head. "I'll have to go back."

Ray swallowed. "What? Are you crazy?"

"Ray, I can't leave the door open. Come help me."

"No way!" Ray cried.

"Come on," Mike insisted. "All you have to do is stand by the front door and hold it open. I'll do the rest. Really. But you've got to stay at the door."

It was the first time Ray had seen his older brother look really scared. "Well . . . okay," he agreed.

Ducking under the hard rain, they ran across the yard to the house. Mike pushed gently on the door. It creaked and swung open slowly. The lights were still on.

"I'll just get the key," he whispered. "That's all I have to do."

Ray held the front door open and watched his brother jog down the hallway to the kitchen.

"Do you remember where you left it?" Ray whispered.

"Yeah. It's on the table."

A deafening crash of thunder froze Mike's steps. The lights flickered twice and went out.

Ray gasped. "Come back, Mike. Forget the stupid key!"

"Don't panic," Mike called. "I've got it. I'm coming back down the hall."

Ray held his breath and waited for his brother. He listened to his soft footsteps on the floor.

"Hey!"

Too many footsteps! Clattering footsteps!

A stampede! Chasing after Mike!

"Run for it!" Mike screamed.

Thunder crashed.

Mike and Ray burst out the door together. Ray slammed the door behind him.

"Hold it shut! Don't let it get out!" Mike shrieked, rain dripping down his frightened face. He fumbled the key in the lock.

The doorknob shook violently in Ray's hand. "What is it? What is it!" Ray cried.

Something pounded the door hard from inside.

"I don't know!" Mike shrieked. "And I don't want to find out!"

Finally, the lock clicked shut. Ray turned to run — but he didn't get far.

A blinding white light trapped them. And they froze.

"The ghost!" Ray choked out.

A deep, angry voice cut through the roar of the storm. "What's going on?" it demanded. "What were you doing in there?"

Ray shielded his eyes. "Mr. Hodge?" he asked hopefully.

"It's the children from next door," a woman's voice said. "We didn't mean to frighten you."

"Mrs. Hodge?" Ray gasped.

Ray and Mike stepped out of the headlights of the Hodges' old car. They saw the couple clearly as they walked toward them.

"We came home early because of the storm." Mr. Hodge grabbed the front doorknob.

"You can't go in there!" Ray screamed. "Something awful is in there. It nearly got us!"

Mrs. Hodge frowned at Mr. Hodge. "I told you we shouldn't have left him." She sounded worried. "He didn't hurt you boys — did he?"

"You know about the gh-ghost?" Mike stammered.

Mr. Hodge shook his head. "Ghost?"

A hard thud on the front door was followed by the high-pitched shriek they'd heard earlier.

Ray covered his ears. His whole body shook.

Mr. Hodge pulled open the front door. And a pink pig came waddling out.

"Walter! You rascal!" Mrs. Hodge cooed. The pig grunted a greeting to her, its snout twitching in the rain.

"He's been our pet for years," Mr. Hodge explained. "But I thought I'd penned him up. When he gets loose, he wrecks the house."

"He's afraid of storms," Mrs. Hodge added. "Goes on a rampage when he hears thunder."

"We know! We know!" Ray exclaimed.

And they all laughed.

At school the next day, Ray and Mike told Chris and the others about their adventure. "So it wasn't a haunted house after all," Ray told them. "The Hodges own a huge pig named Walter."

The girl with braces looked puzzled. "*Everyone* knows about the Hodges and Walter," she said. "Their house isn't haunted. It's the one next door. The empty one, on the left."

"No, it's not!" Chris argued. "It's the house on the *right*."

"Huh? The house on the right?" Ray choked out.

"Yes. The one on the right," Chris repeated. "The one with the crooked chimney." He turned to the girl with braces. "Don't you know your left from your right?"

"Oh, yeah. You're right," the girl agreed. "The house on the right. Everyone knows that house is filled with ghosts. Very angry ghosts. Very dangerous ghosts."

"No one ever survives in that house," another boy added, shaking his head.

Chris turned back to Ray and Mike. "By the way, where do you guys live?" he asked.

FUN WITH SPELLING

The cab honked for the third time.

"Aunt Vera, your cab is waiting!" I called.

Aunt Vera rushed down the stairs, lugging her beat-up old suitcase. She wore a huge straw hat, a baggy sundress, and white socks with sandals.

And she wore the disgusting garlic necklace she always wore. She said the garlic kept away evil spirits.

Aunt Vera is so weird, with all her talk about spells and curses.

"I asked the travel spirits about this flight," she said in her Southern accent. "They said today was a good day to fly."

I glanced at my mom. She rolled her eyes and smiled at me.

"Take care, Vera," Mom said, giving her a big hug.

Libby, my eight-year-old sister, jumped up into Aunt Vera's arms and kissed her on the cheek. She's always trying to act cute.

Libby and I both have curly brown hair and freckles. But her hair is cut short, so the curls bounce around her face. Everyone says that Libby looks like a little doll.

They don't know her the way I do.

"Thanks for sharing your room with me, Kari," Aunt Vera said to me. "I hope I didn't bother you with all my chanting."

"No problem," I lied. "Have a good trip."

As soon as Aunt Vera left, I ran up to my room to air it out. Aunt Vera wore that gross garlic necklace all week long, and it really made my room stink.

I opened all my windows as wide as they would go. Now that Aunt Vera was gone, I could go back to my normal life. Mom made me keep my room clean and neat for Aunt Vera. What a pain. I'm not used to picking my stuff up all the time.

I tore through my junk, searching for my book on magic. My friend Toby teases me about always having a new hobby. One week it's painting. The next week it's stamp collecting.

It's just that I get so bored, I have to start something new.

My new hobby is magic.

I found a half-eaten candy bar, a bag of pretzels, and a book I had been looking for — but no magic book. I was about to give up when I saw something sticking out from under my pillow.

I pulled out a small, leather-bound book and studied it. The title, MAGIC SPELLS AND SORCERY, was in gold letters on the cover.

It sure wasn't my dumb little book of magic tricks. This book looked really old.

I opened it and saw my aunt's scratchy handwriting across the title page:

DEAR KARI,

I HOPE YOU FIND THIS BOOK USEFUL. THANKS AGAIN FOR SHARING YOUR ROOM WITH ME.

MAY THE GOOD SPIRITS SHINE ON YOU!

LOVE,

AUNT VERA

May the good spirits shine on you?

What a wacko!

I skimmed the Table of Contents. Weather Spells, Love Spells, Beauty Spells, Enemy Spells . . .

Enemy Spells? *Cool!*

I turned to that page right away.

Dozens of spells filled the pages. There was everything from causing people to go bald to making their teeth fall out.

"What are you doing?"

I spun around. My nosy sister stood in my doorway.

"I told you not to come into my room!" I shouted.

"I'm not in your room," Libby argued. "I'm in the hallway."

"Well, you're way too close," I said. "Go away. This isn't baby stuff."

She stuck her tongue out at me. "Who would want to go in your smelly room, anyway? Yuck!" She held her nose.

I slammed the door in her face and went back to my book.

I ran my finger over the spells. Aging Spell. Wart-Growing Spell. As soon as I saw the Forgetfulness Spell, I knew what I had to do.

Lisa McFly. It was perfect for her.

Lisa McFly is the meanest girl in the entire sixth grade. Once, she put a dead bird in my desk. Another time she told everyone I was in love with Timmy Wardell. Yuck! Everyone *hates* Timmy Wardell, including me!

Lisa loves spreading rumors and saying mean things about people.

Lisa prides herself on her perfect clothes, perfect hair, and perfect grades. She's never late for class, and she never forgets her homework. It's enough to make you puke.

I read the Forgetfulness Spell. It probably wouldn't work. But, still, it was worth a try. Lisa McFly definitely deserved it.

"First," I read, "write your enemy's name on a piece of paper. Place the paper in a glass jar. Then spit in the jar and seal it tightly."

I found an old jelly jar I kept change in. Then I wrote Lisa's name on a piece of paper and stuffed it inside, along with a big gob of spit. Then I returned to the instructions:

"Face north and chant the following phrase three times:

> By morning when the sun is shining
> your enemy will forget
> the one thing that is most important
> which he or she will truly regret."

Then I had to place the jar on my windowsill, "where the moonlight would touch it."

Later, while I was lying in bed, I thought about how stupid the whole thing was. Forgetfulness spell! What a waste of time.

I stared at the jar on my windowsill. The moonlight shimmered on the glass.

Was the jar *glowing*?

The next day, I showed up at math class early. Math is first period. I'm usually the last one in. But today I was curious about my spell.

Lisa walked in wearing her perfect hair in a perfect braid down her back. She slid into the chair next to mine.

When Mr. Pratt asked everyone for their homework, I held my breath. Would Lisa forget hers?

Don't be crazy, I scolded myself. There's no way. Little Miss Perfect would never forget anything.

I ripped my homework out of my notebook while I watched Lisa. She looked puzzled as she searched through every page of her notebook. She held up her textbook and shook it.

I handed my homework to Mr. Pratt. He stood near Lisa's desk, waiting for her. "Lisa," he said, "where's your homework?"

Lisa leafed frantically through her notebook again. She dug through her backpack, tossing papers and pencils on the floor. She was in a total panic.

I glanced over at my friend Toby. He had a huge grin on his face.

"I — I can't find it," Lisa stammered. "I must have forgotten it. I don't know what happened."

"Get it to me by tomorrow," Mr. Pratt said sternly. "And let's make sure this doesn't happen again."

My heart thudded so hard, I thought it might explode. My spell — it worked! It really worked!

"That's too bad about your homework, Lisa," I whispered to her.

Lisa sneered at me. "Get lost, geek."

She really shouldn't have said that. Now I *had* to try another spell on her.

Later in my room, I studied the Enemy Spells

chapter, searching for the perfect one. Something really embarrassing. Something so bad, Lisa would wish she had never come to school that day.

Then I found it.

The *perfect* spell.

It was going to make school history!

Lisa strolled into math class a few minutes early the next morning. She handed Mr. Pratt her homework. She stood by his desk with a sickening-sweet smile on her face.

"Thank you, Lisa," Mr. Pratt said.

Lisa opened her mouth to say something to him.

This was it! The true test of Aunt Vera's spell book. I held my breath — and waited for her to speak.

"UUUUURRRRRPP!"

Lisa burped. A deafening burp that practically shook the walls.

Yes! The spell worked!

Mr. Pratt's mouth hung open. For a few seconds, everyone in class was completely quiet. Then we all cracked up.

"Lisa, are you all right?" Mr. Pratt asked.

Lisa's face turned bright red. She opened her mouth to speak again.

"UUUUURRRRRPP!"

The second burp was even louder than the first. We all laughed so hard, Mr. Pratt had to bang the chalkboard with his ruler.

"Quiet, please! Quiet!" Mr. Pratt shouted.

The class was out of control. Toby laughed so hard, he fell off his chair.

Lisa held both hands over her mouth. I could see tiny beads of sweat on her forehead.

"What did you have for breakfast, Lisa? Beans?" Mike Shea called out to her.

Lisa glared at him. She opened her mouth once more.

"UUUURRRPP!"

Lisa's eyes bulged out of her head. She turned to face Mr. Pratt. By now he was laughing too.

My stomach ached from laughing so hard. I could barely breathe.

Lisa ran out of the room. We could hear her burp as she ran down the hall into the bathroom.

What a day! Lisa's burping was the talk of the school.

When I saw Lisa during lunch, I had to say something to her. I couldn't wait to hear her burp again.

"Are you sure you want to drink that Coke, Lisa?" I asked her. "It could be trouble."

Lisa curled her lip. "Gee, that's so funny I forgot to laugh."

Huh?

She didn't burp. The spell must have worn off.

Too bad, I thought. Maybe I'll cast a new spell on her. Something even worse.

I was dying to tell Toby about my spells. But I knew he'd never believe me. Besides, Toby has such a big mouth. I didn't want Lisa to find out who was casting them. Not yet, at least.

"Did you *believe* Lisa McFly today?" I asked Toby on the way home.

Toby giggled. "Yeah. I bet she wished she could 'McFly' right out of the room!"

That gave me a great idea.

As soon as I got home, I hurried up the stairs to my room, smiling to myself.

My next spell was going to be a masterpiece.

I stopped at the top of the stairs. The door to my room was open.

Strange. I always keep the door closed.

I ran inside to look for the spell book in my desk drawer.

Gone!

How could that be?

I began ripping through my desk drawers, dumping each one out on the floor. I tore apart my closet, tossing things over my shoulder as I dug to the bottom of the pile.

"Libby!" I screamed. "Get in here!"

Libby appeared at the door. She kept her eyes on the floor. She looked very guilty.

"Did you take something from my room?" I demanded.

"No," she replied.

"Are you sure?" I asked. Libby is a champion liar.

"I'm *positive*," she insisted.

I yanked up the dust ruffle to my bed.

Found it! How did it get down there?

"Hey, what's that?" Libby asked innocently.

"None of your business," I snapped. "Don't slam the door on your way out."

She slammed the door, of course.

I paged to the chapter called *Creating Your Own Spells*. It said: "Write on a piece of paper what you want your enemy to do, and add it to the jar."

I took a fresh piece of paper out of my notebook. I wrote: TOMORROW, WHEN LISA MCFLY HEARS HER NAME, I WANT HER TO THINK SHE CAN REALLY FLY. I stuffed the paper into the jar.

This was going to be great!

The next morning, everyone was quiet when Lisa strutted into the classroom. She tried to act as cool as ever, but I could tell she was nervous by the way she bit her lip.

Lisa opened up her notebook as soon as she sat down, as if there were some incredibly interesting message inside. She kept her head down as Mr. Pratt read the roll call.

I held my breath until he got to her name. "Lisa McFly."

Lisa's head jerked up at the sound of her name. Would my new spell work?

Lisa slowly got up from her chair. She stretched her arms to her sides — and started flapping them like wings!

"Lisa? What is the matter with you?" Mr. Pratt demanded.

Lisa flapped her arms even harder.

Toby burst out laughing. Then we all laughed like crazy watching Lisa flap her arms.

"Lisa McFly thinks she can fly! Lisa McFly thinks she can fly!" we all chanted.

Each time Lisa heard her name, she flapped her arms even harder.

Mr. Pratt banged on the chalkboard, but it was no use. Kids shrieked with laughter as they chanted and laughed at Lisa.

Then an amazing thing happened.

Lisa actually raised herself up from the floor.

She flapped her arms frantically — and raised herself higher and higher. Soon she was two feet off the ground!

"Whoa! Wait a minute!" I cried. "She's really flying!"

Everyone stopped chanting and clapping. Mr. Pratt dropped his ruler.

Lisa floated to the open window, her arms flapping furiously.

Our classroom was three stories up!

"Stop her!" I shouted. "She'll fall!"

Toby and I raced to the window. Toby grabbed her around her waist. I held her feet.

"Lisa, stop! It's only a joke! You can't really fly!" I cried.

But Lisa kept flapping her arms harder and harder, trying to break away from us.

"I don't know how much longer I can hold her!" Toby cried.

Mr. Pratt rushed over and tried to hold Lisa down.

"Come on, everyone! Help!" I shouted.

Lisa kicked and thrashed as we struggled to hold her down.

I knew I had to break the spell! Before it was too late!

I remembered a chapter in the book about breaking spells. I let go of Lisa's feet and ran to the door.

"Hold her down!" I called. "I'll be right back!"

I raced to my house with only one thing on my mind. Break the spell! I had to break the spell!

I took the stairs two at a time and burst into my room.

I ripped the room apart. Where was it? Where *was* it?

"LIBBY YOU LITTLE CREEP DID YOU TAKE MY —"

My body suddenly froze. I felt a strange tingle run up and down my back.

"What's happen —"

My right leg twitched. Then my left.

I did a back-flip!

"UUUUUUURRRPPP!"

I burped! A long, gross burp from deep in my stomach.

What was happening to me?

I back-flipped again. I couldn't stop myself. I back-flipped out of my room and into the hallway.

"What's — UUURRRRRRPPPPP!"

I flipped and burped my way into Libby's room.

Libby sat on her bed. Was that the magic book in her lap? Why wasn't she at school yet?

"Did you cast a spell on me?" That's what I wanted to ask her. But all that came out was a disgusting "URRRRRRP."

I tried again. "URRRRP."

I heard a flapping sound at the window. Libby and I both turned — and watched Lisa fly into the room.

"Thanks, Libby," Lisa said, grinning.

"Hey. No problem," Libby replied.

"URRRRRRRP!" I replied. And did another back-flip.

MATT'S LUNCH BOX

My name is Matt Green, and I don't usually forget things. But this happens to be the first day of spring. And baseball tryouts are this afternoon.

So is it my fault I left my dumb lunch box on the bus?

I didn't even realize it until I reached my house. I was heading to my room to find my mitt. On the way, I passed Mom in the kitchen.

"Hi, Matt," she called out. "How was your day?"

"Fine," I said. I was thinking about how hard it would be to beat out Todd Fisher for catcher.

"How about a snack?" Mom asked.

"I'm not hungry, Mom."

"Are you sure, Matt?" she called after me. "How about some cookies?"

"No, thanks." Mom is always trying to force me to eat. She thinks I'm too skinny.

I ran to my room, grabbed my mitt, and headed for the front door.

In the kitchen, Mom waved an apple at me. "You really should eat something," she said.

"Okay." I shoved the apple into my jacket.

"Did you finish your lunch today?"

"Oh, no!" I suddenly remembered my lunch box. "Sorry. I just left my lunch box on the bus."

Mom frowned. "Can you get it back?"

"I don't think so." I sighed. "There's no such thing as Bus Lost and Found."

Mom shook her head. "I guess I'll have to buy another one then."

I left for tryouts and didn't think about my lunch box again. Then today, Mom shoved a bright red plastic rectangular box into my hands. "Surprise!"

"What's this?" I asked.

"A new lunch box," she replied.

I made a face. "Mom! You call this a lunch box?"

"What's wrong with it?"

I pointed to the stupid cartoon on the front. "This is for a little kid. I don't want a lunch box with flying monsters on it. Everyone will make fun of me! Why couldn't you get me a plain lunch box like the last one?"

Mom frowned. "This happens to be the ONLY lunch box I could find this time of year," she said. "Every place is sold out. I went to four stores."

It was so dumb looking. The monsters were

about the size of parakeets. Each one had a set of leathery wings and long, sharp teeth.

They reminded me of bats or gargoyles.

I took the lunch box to my room and slammed the door behind me.

I threw myself down on the bed and stared angrily at the picture on the front.

The three monsters glared back at me. Their red bug eyes seemed to glitter and flash. Their jagged teeth and tiny clawed hands and feet looked as sharp as razors.

Then I noticed something else. The little creatures were flying out of a lunch box exactly the same as the one I was holding. And they were chasing some poor kid across a kitchen. His mouth was open wide, screaming.

A strange feeling came over me. Maybe I shouldn't open this lunch box, I thought. It was really giving me the creeps.

It's just a dumb old lunch box, I told myself.

I slowly cracked open the lid.

I heard a tiny voice. "We're hungry, Matt. Let us out."

"Huh?" I slammed the lid shut. The voice stopped!

My hands were shaking now. Something inside that lunch box knew my name! But how could that be?

I put the lunch box on the shelf above my desk.

Then I grabbed my mitt and ran out to baseball practice.

When I reached the field, Coach Goldberg waved me over. "Congratulations, Green," he said. "You're starting catcher."

"I am? Wow!" I quickly put on my mask and pads and forgot all about my lunch box.

Around midnight a noise woke me. I sprang up in bed. What was it?

Something was knocking inside my lunch box!

I stared in disbelief. The lunch box was still right where I left it, on the shelf above my desk. But now it was actually shaking and moving.

"Who is it? What do you want?" I choked out.

The knocking grew louder. "Let us out, Matt," a voice cried from inside. "We're hungry!"

I pulled my covers up over my chin. I was too afraid to move.

The lunch box rocked harder. It edged forward on the shelf until half of it hung over.

Then it toppled over. It smashed onto my desk with a loud thud.

I gasped. The lid popped open — and three monsters flew out!

"Whoa! Help!" I shouted.

The monsters zoomed toward me, flapping their leathery wings.

"Chow time!" screamed the biggest one.

The monsters circled closer. They all had jagged teeth and crinkled skin. "Food! We want food!" the big one screamed.

"I don't have any food!" I cried.

A middle-sized monster flipped a few somersaults in the air. He pointed at me and laughed. "You don't get it, do you? You have to feed us, Matt." He chomped his teeth and rolled his red bug eyes backwards. "Whoever owns the lunch box owns us. We belong to you now."

"That's right," a little one screeched. "And we're starved."

They roared over to my dresser.

"Hey! What are you doing?" I yelled. "Stop that!"

The three monsters used their claws to pry open my top dresser drawer. "Where's our food, Matt?" the big one demanded.

They started tossing my clothes onto the floor.

"Where do you hide your candy?" the little one said. "I want candy!"

"I don't hide candy!" I shouted.

"Liar!" the middle one yelled. He rolled his bug eyes backwards again, then curled his top lip back. "Let's try the closet!"

"Stop it!" I cried. They shot inside. I ducked as an old Monopoly game and a pair of sneakers zinged past.

A squeaky voice cried out, "Food!"

Seconds later, they were dragging my bag of

leftover Halloween candy out. I'd forgotten I even had it.

The monsters threw the bag on the floor and gobbled up the few stale pieces that were there, including the wrappings.

"Where's the rest?" the big one demanded.

"I didn't get enough," the little one whined. "I never get enough."

"There isn't any more," I said. "Please stop."

The monsters turned angrily to me. "You have to feed us," the middle one said. "Now."

"But . . . I don't have any food," I told them.

"Then we'll eat *you*," the biggest one shrieked. He charged toward me with his mouth wide open.

"No!" I raised my arm to try to stop him. He sank his fangs into my arm.

"Owww!" I screamed. He pulled his fangs from my skin. I could see a gash where he'd bitten me. He was serious.

I ran out the door and down the hall. "Mom!" I screamed. "Help me!"

The big one cut me off. "I wouldn't do that if I were you." He bared his teeth again.

"Be right back," I said. I raced to the kitchen and threw open the cupboards. Crackers, cookies, pretzels, cereal. I grabbed everything I could find, including the rice cakes.

I dashed back to my room and threw the food on my bed. "Here. Now, leave me alone."

"FOOOOD!" they cried. They fell onto it

greedily. The big one started shoving chocolate-chip cookies into his mouth.

"Stop being such a pig!" the little one screamed. "You always hog the food."

The middle one was cramming pretzels down his throat so fast, I thought he'd choke.

It took them less than three minutes to finish everything. Then, as soon as they were done, they quickly vanished.

Breathing hard, I stood and waited for a moment. Were they going to come back?

When they didn't return, I crept into bed and pulled the covers up to my head. The lunch box was still sitting on my desk. I watched it until I fell asleep.

The next morning I tiptoed over to the lunch box and peeked inside. Empty.

I heard my mother calling me. "Matt! Breakfast!"

With a flap of wings, three monsters came flying out of my closet. "Feed us. Feed us," the little one whined.

The middle one was spinning somersaults in the air. "I love bacon and eggs, Matt. Is that what we're having? Huh? Huh?"

I ran down the hall, the monsters close behind me. "Mom!" I yelled. I burst into the kitchen and ran to her side. "They're after me!"

"Who?"

"*They* are!" I spun around and pointed at . . . nothing!

"I don't see anything, Matt," Mom said.

Nothing there.

Mom pointed to the plate of scrambled eggs and bacon in front of me. "Sit down and eat your breakfast before it gets cold."

I slumped into my chair. I picked up my fork and started to take a bite of egg.

The little monster swooped down from the fridge and landed on my fork. "Hi, Matt," he whispered. "Don't tell Fatso I'm starting without him."

I gasped. "But — that's mi —" Before I could finish, the little monster gobbled up my bite — and everything else on my plate.

"Mom — look!" I shouted. Too late.

Mom turned around. The monster had already disappeared. She gave me a huge smile. "Matt! Done already?"

My words rushed out. "Mom. I didn't eat it! It was the monsters. They came with my lunch box. If I don't feed them, they'll eat us!"

Mom gave me a hug. "It's okay," she said, laughing. "I'm glad to see you're finally getting a good appetite. Now I know who sneaked in here and ate all those crackers and cookies last night!"

At noon, I sat down for lunch in the cafeteria. My lunch box was empty. Licked clean.

I slammed the lid back down. My stomach growled. I hadn't eaten since dinner the night before.

What was I going to do?

By afternoon, I was really hungry. I couldn't wait to go home and have a snack. When I stepped off the bus, I ran as fast as I could into my house. I threw open the cabinets and pulled down a huge bag of chips.

I ripped open the bag. But just as my fingers hit the first chip, the lunch-box monsters showed up.

"No," I cried, backing up. "Stay away."

"We're hungry, Matt," the middle one said.

I clutched the bag to my chest. "No. It's mine. You *had* lunch."

"Drop the bag, Matt," the big monster yelled. He started jabbing at my fingers with the sharp points of his teeth.

"Ow!" I dropped the bag on the floor, spilling chips everywhere. The monsters moved in. Seconds later, the chips were gone.

"Please," I begged. "Just let me have a little something."

The middle monster turned another somersault and laughed. "Sorry, Matt. When we're full, it's your turn."

"And we're never full!" The little one laughed.

Tired and weak, I dragged myself up to my room. If only I could eat. . . .

The next thing I knew, Mom was calling me to dinner. I must have been so weak from hunger that I fell asleep!

I managed to make it into the kitchen. Mom had cooked up another feast — juicy roast beef, scalloped potatoes, green beans, rolls, fresh apple pie.

I smacked my lips. Mmmm. I slid into my chair, smiling. Food . . . food . . . food.

"Go ahead and start," Mom called from across the kitchen. I hungrily picked up my fork and started to dig into my potatoes. Suddenly the big monster was flapping over my fork.

He swooped down and ate my potatoes. Beside him, the little monster gobbled up my beans. And the middle monster grabbed the roast beef and swallowed it whole!

Mom turned around. She glanced down at my empty plate. "Would you like seconds?"

I had an idea. "Mom, I'll take seconds if you come eat with me." The monsters wouldn't be able to steal my food if Mom was watching!

"No, dear. I had a big lunch. I'll eat later."

"Mom, please," I begged. "Come sit with me."

"Honey, I'm really busy."

"Fine!" I shouted. "Then I'll just starve to death, okay?"

I stomped upstairs and threw myself on my bed. I stared at the ceiling and thought about hamburgers.

Around midnight, my growling stomach woke me up. I got out of bed and sneaked down the hall in the dark to the kitchen. Maybe the monsters were asleep.

I tore open the cupboard and pulled out a giant bag of cookies. Before I even opened it, the big monster swooped in and snatched it out of my hand.

"No!" I screamed.

"Why can't you leave me alone? You've eaten plenty today."

He jammed a fistful of cookies into his mouth. "What are you talking about?" he said. "All I had was potatoes."

"STOP!" I screamed. I grabbed the cookie bag and ran.

The other two flew down from the cupboards and tried to pull the bag from my hands.

"No! Please!" I begged. "If I don't eat soon . . ." But they took the bag and gobbled it up.

Upset and weak, I dragged myself back to bed.

In the morning I felt so exhausted, I didn't want to get out of bed. Even dressing was tough. Finally, I pulled myself to the breakfast table. Mom had fixed French toast and sausage.

I could see Mom watching me as I sat down. "What's wrong, Matt?" she said. "You look awful."

"I haven't eaten for two days!" I cried. "I told

you. There are little monsters who came from my lunch box. And they won't let me eat."

"Now, Matt. We both know that's not true." She put her hand on my forehead. "No fever."

It was hopeless. She was never going to believe me. No one was.

I watched the monsters enjoy my breakfast. Then I picked up my backpack.

I was so weak, I wasn't even sure I could make it to the bus stop. I had to get rid of the monsters before it was too late. But how?

Suddenly I remembered something. They had said they belong to the person who owns the lunch box.

If only there was some way to get rid of the lunch box.

At the corner I saw a sign in a neighbor's yard: FIVE-FAMILY TAG SALE TODAY. Then I noticed a sign on one of the tag-sale tables: EVERYTHING HERE 50¢.

Maybe this was my answer! No one would even know.

I walked past the 50¢ table a couple of times until I was sure no one was watching. I slowly reached into my backpack and pulled out the lunch box. One more glance around. Okay . . . NOW!

I dropped the lunch box on the table. Then I ran to some nearby bushes and hid. A few minutes later, I saw a lady pick up the lunch box. She turned it over in her hands a few times.

Would she buy it? Come on, lady. Fifty cents — a real bargain!

She took two quarters out of her wallet. She handed the money to the cashier. "Thank you," the cashier said. "Enjoy your lunch box."

I couldn't believe it. It was that easy. I was rid of my lunch box. No monsters to steal my food. I was free! Free!

I turned around.

Using my last bit of strength, I slumped back to my house. Weak and dazed, I threw open the refrigerator door and collapsed on the floor. I reached up, grabbed a pear, and shoved it in my mouth.

I began to chew. I swallowed a bite. Then another. And another.

I ate until I was sick to my stomach. I couldn't believe how great everything tasted. I had to walk to school because I had missed my bus. But so what?

Later, during dinner, I was reaching for my fourth helping when the doorbell rang. Mom went to answer. I heard her say, "Murray! What a nice surprise!"

My uncle Murray is Mom's brother. He's a traveling salesman. Whenever he's in town, he stops by.

Uncle Murray came into the kitchen carrying his briefcase and a large plastic bag. "Hi, Matt. I brought you something!"

"I hope it's something to eat," I joked.

"Sort of," Uncle Murray said. "Your mom mentioned you lost your lunch box the other day, so . . ."

I frantically waved my arms. "No . . . no! I don't need a lunch box! No lunch box!"

"Matt!" Mom cried. "What's gotten into you?"

"Don't worry, Matt," Uncle Murray said. "Your mom told me she bought you a great lunch box already. But . . ."

He reached into the plastic bag — and pulled out a red thermos. "She said you still needed to find the matching thermos!"

My mouth dropped open.

"Can you believe it, Matt?" Mom said. "It's the very same design as your lunch box."

I stared in horror.

No! It couldn't be!

As I stared, the little monster peeked out and winked at me. "Boy, am I thirsty!" he whispered.

STUCK IN 1957

"Perfect," Shanna murmured.

She sat in the backseat of the car, checking her auburn hair in a mirror. It fell to her shoulders. Her bangs were the perfect length.

Yesterday at Chic Cuts, the hairstylist had talked her into layering the back. Shanna loved it! She had to admit it — she had great hair!

"Does it hurt, Shanna?" her nine-year-old brother asked.

"Huh?" Shanna glanced over at David. "Does what hurt?"

"Your face!" David cried. "'Cause it's killing me!"

"If only," Shanna muttered. Her thoughts drifted back to her hair.

Great hair was important, because tomorrow, Shanna Smith was going to be the new girl in seventh grade at Westwood Middle School. Deep inside she knew that if her hair looked great, everything else would be great too.

Shanna gazed into the mirror. "Perfect," she murmured again.

"What's perfect, Shanna?" her mom asked. She pulled the car into the driveway of their new house.

The moving van had delivered their furniture that morning. Now the Smiths had to unpack.

"Oh, uh, nothing," Shanna replied. She tucked away her mirror and glanced at their new house. It was part brick and part wood, painted blue.

"To think this house was built when I was a boy, back in nineteen fifty-seven!" Shanna's father exclaimed. "It still looks brand new."

David hopped out of the car and ran up the sidewalk to unlock the door. Shanna and her parents climbed out of the car.

"It must have been so cool to grow up in the fifties, Dad," Shanna said. "Elvis. Hula hoops. Rock and roll."

"It wasn't all rock and roll," her dad replied. He opened the trunk and handed her a suitcase. "Unpack fast," he ordered. "It's almost five-thirty. We're due at Aunt Gigi's for dinner at six."

"No way!" Shanna cried. "I can't go."

"Why?" mom asked her. "You have other plans?"

Shanna rolled her eyes. "I have to wash my hair. I always wash it the day after I get it cut. I really have to!"

"Can't you do it in the morning?" asked her dad.

"I have to do this super-conditioning treatment on it tonight," she explained. "Or it won't work in the morning."

Shanna carried her suitcase down the hall to her new room. She flung it onto her bed. She snapped it open and started to unpack.

She opened a drawer to put away her socks. "Hey — what's this?" she muttered to herself. She pulled out a pair of glasses. "Someone must have left these behind."

They had black plastic frames that curved up on the outside edges. Little rhinestones were set into the frames. Cat Woman glasses, Shanna thought. Cool!

Shanna faced the mirror and slipped the glasses on. Wow! She looked so fifties! Like a character from *Grease*!

But — whoa!

What was the funny tingling feeling in her head?

Why was her face wobbling in the mirror like that? Why was the room spinning? Why did she feel dizzy and sick to her stomach?

Shanna slumped onto her bed. She lay there with her eyes shut until the dizzy feeling lifted. Then she opened her eyes and sat up.

Her room looked . . . different. Sort of lived in.

She picked up a pink pillow. Sparkly silver letters on it spelled out ELVIS.

Shanna put the pillow down. Why hadn't she

noticed it before? And why hadn't she noticed the ugly black dial phone by her bed? The pink bedspread? The frilly pink curtains?

Shanna gasped. She hadn't noticed because — a minute ago — they weren't there!

Shanna sprang up. She ran over to the mirror.

She swiped the glasses off. Her face wasn't wobbling now. That was good. And her hair looked perfect. Nothing was wrong.

What could be wrong?

Shanna turned to finish unpacking. But her suitcase was gone.

She glanced at the closet and gasped. She ran over to it. Her clothes had vanished! Hanging in their place were aqua pedal pushers. Beaded sweaters. A peach-colored blouse and skirt. A pink poodle skirt!

All the clothes looked like stuff she'd seen in a fifties magazine. Like the fifties rack at the thrift shop!

What was going on? Shanna checked her watch. Five-thirty. But the seconds weren't ticking off. Her watch had stopped!

"Shanna?" a voice called.

"Coming, Mom!" Shanna called. She ran out the door of her room and down the hall. She burst into the kitchen. And stopped.

At the counter stood a woman Shanna had never seen before. Her blond hair was swept up into a big heap on her head. She wore an apron over a pink-and-white-checked dress. She had on high heels. She looked ready to go to a fifties costume party!

Who *was* she?

"Shanna, dear!" the woman exclaimed. "What are you wearing?"

"Me?" Shanna cried. She had on a pair of jeans and a purple T-shirt. So what? She wasn't the weird one! This woman was!

"Are you in a play at school, dear?" the woman asked. "Are you supposed to be some crazy outer-space creature?"

"What are you talking about?" Shanna cried. "Who are you?"

"Oh, are those your lines from the play?" the woman asked. "Now go back to your room and put on a skirt for dinner, dear."

Shanna's heart began to race. She hurried back to her room. She closed the door behind her.

There on her dresser stood the black Cat Woman glasses. She picked them up. Had *they* brought her here? She'd put the glasses on and *whoosh*! Had she really time-traveled to the fifties?

If she had, then the glasses should work in reverse — right?

All she had to do was put them on again. And *WHOOSH*! She'd be back to the right year.

She pulled them out. She started to put them back on. Then she stopped.

96

Hey! she thought. Maybe I shouldn't go back right away. Maybe I should hang around and check things out for a while.

Now that Shanna had figured out what happened — and how to get back — she didn't feel so scared.

Alive in the fifties! Suddenly it seemed totally cool!

Shanna smiled. She changed into a white beaded sweater, a pink poodle skirt, white socks, and saddle shoes.

She checked the mirror on the back of her closet door and giggled. Pretty goofy clothes! But fun!

She slipped the Cat Woman glasses into her skirt pocket. That way, she could return to her family anytime she wanted.

Shanna hurried into the dining room. There at the table sat the woman, a man in a suit and tie, and a boy.

The woman called the boy Davy. He looked around nine. He had on a ratty fur cap. A raccoon tail hung down the back of his neck.

Gross! Shanna thought. A Davy Crockett hat.

The dinner was totally disgusting. Some big hunk of dried-out meat. Overcooked green beans. Canned pineapple salad.

"Where's your appetite?" the woman asked Shanna.

"I'm not hungry now," Shanna said. "Maybe

later I'll grab a juice box and nuke a burrito in the micro."

"You'll do *what*?" the man exclaimed.

"Shanna is in a play, darling," the woman told the man.

Shanna choked down dinner.

Afterwards, everybody went into the living room. They watched a movie about a talking mule on a tiny black-and-white TV. Everybody thought it was really funny.

Everybody but Shanna. "Who's got the zapper?" she asked.

"The what?" asked Davy.

"The remote. You know," Shanna said. "To change channels?"

"Are those more lines from your play?" the woman asked.

"Uh . . . never mind," Shanna said. How was she supposed to know remotes weren't around in 1957?

The next morning, Shanna walked into the kitchen wearing a white blouse and a cool pair of black pedal pushers.

"Good morning," she said to the woman.

The woman gasped. "It's a school day, dear!" she said. "You know you have to wear a skirt. Hurry and change."

Shanna hurried upstairs and came back down in a powder-blue skirt and matching blouse.

"That's better," said the woman. She patted a

stool by the kitchen counter. "Hop up here for a minute."

Shanna hopped, and the woman picked up a pair of scissors.

"Hey, what are you doing with those?" Shanna began. "HEY!"

"Those bangs of yours are so long," the woman said. "They're hiding your pretty brown eyes."

"Don't touch my hair with those things!" Shanna screamed.

But she heard a *SNIP*!

"Just a trim," the woman said. "Stop squirming."

She snipped another hunk of Shanna's hair. And another.

Shanna froze. This woman was clearly a maniac!

But, wait. Shanna didn't have to put up with this. There was something she could do!

She reached into her pocket and pulled out the Cat Woman glasses.

"ENOUGH!" Shanna roared. She shoved on the glasses.

Would they work? Would they take her forward to her time? Return her to her family?

No.

Nothing happened. No tingling. Nothing.

She took the glasses off. She put them on again.

Nothing.

Her heart began to pound. What could be wrong with the glasses?

"Settle down, Shanna," the woman said, snipping away. "There," she added, stepping back. "All done!"

Shanna put a hand to her forehead. She moved her fingers up. *Way* up! Up by her hairline, she felt some prickly little stubs.

"What have you *done*?" Shanna shrieked. She jumped off the stool and ran to the bathroom. She stared into the mirror and gasped.

It was worse than she'd imagined. She looked like a total freak!

Shanna took out the black glasses again. She put them on every which way. Upside down. Right side up. With her eyes crossed.

But she felt no tingling.

The truth finally hit her. She was stuck in 1957!

What can I do? Shanna wondered. Her panic made her dizzy. She wanted to shut her eyes — and open them back in her new house with her family, in her own time.

Will I ever see my parents again? she wondered.

A few minutes later, Shanna found herself on a school bus. She looked around at ponytailed girls in calf-length skirts. And boys with buzz cuts and plaid shirts.

At least no one stared at her. At least she

wasn't the only short-banged freak having a bad-hair day.

"Hi, Shanna!" a girl with strawberry-blond hair called as Shanna stepped down from the bus. She fell into step beside Shanna and walked with her into school.

Shanna stuck with her and entered a class-room. A stout woman in a blue plaid dress sat behind the teacher's desk.

"Good morning, Miss Huntley," the girl said.

"Good morning, Jan," the teacher said. "Shanna."

Jan sat in the front row. Shanna took the desk beside her.

She took her Cat Woman glasses out of her pocket. She put them on. But she felt nothing. And all she saw through the lenses was Miss Huntley, passing out a math test.

At lunch, Shanna and Jan sat together at a long table in the cafeteria. Shanna pushed beets and gray meat around on her plate. Ugh! Where was the pizza? The tacos? The salad bar?

"Look!" Jan whispered as a man with a crew cut walked by their table. "There's Mr. Bolton, the cute new science teacher."

Science, Shanna thought. She watched the teacher sit down at a table of boys. Maybe science could help her get home again!

"I'm so glad he has cafeteria duty this week!" Jan giggled.

"I'll be back." Shanna stood up and walked over to Mr. Bolton's table.

"Excuse me, Mr. Bolton?" Shanna bent down level with him. "I have to talk to you," she whispered. "It's an emergency."

"All right," the teacher said. "What is the matter?"

Shanna glanced around at the boys. They were all ears. Especially one nerdy boy with big teeth.

She dropped her voice. "It's . . . it's about time-travel," she whispered. "Um . . . I came here from the future. But I'm stuck. I can't get back!"

Mr. Bolton frowned. "Stick to your project on levers and pulleys," he instructed. "Time-travel would be a science-*fiction* project, Shanna. Now, run along."

"But, please! I'm desperate!" Shanna cried. "I don't belong here! I — I'm trapped!"

But the teacher didn't hear her. He had turned back to the boys at the table, who were all talking at once.

Shanna slunk away. "Trapped," she murmured. "Trapped."

When the three-thirty bell rang, Shanna thought it was the best sound she'd ever heard. As she walked out of school with Jan, the boy with the big teeth came up to them.

"What do you want, Marvin?" Jan asked.

"I heard what you said about time-travel," he told Shanna.

"Beat it, Marvin!" Jan said. "You are so weird!"

"Only trying to help." Marvin turned and began walking away.

"Marvin, wait!" Shanna cried. "What about time-travel?"

Marvin stopped. He smiled. "I — I have something you might want to see," he said. "It's at my house."

"Okay," Shanna said. "Let's go. Where do you live?"

"Are you crazy, Shanna?" Jan cried. "Would you really go to Marvin's house? Ugh!"

Shanna sighed. "I have to tell you something, Jan. I'm not the Shanna you think I am. I'm Shanna from the future."

"Huh?" Jan only stared at her.

But Marvin grinned his toothy grin. "Sometimes I think I'm from another *planet*," he confessed.

"Shanna, I'm going home," Jan said. "Are you coming or not?"

"Not, I guess," Shanna said.

"Well!" Jan said huffily. "I hope you and Marvin have a good time!" She whirled around and stomped off.

Shanna and Marvin walked two blocks in silence. They stopped outside an old house. Shanna saw that it was right behind her new house.

"What I want to show you is in the shed," Marvin said.

They cut through Marvin's yard to a rickety old toolshed. Marvin pushed open the door. A bare lightbulb on the ceiling clicked on.

Marvin banged around and picked up a metal helmet. He blew dust from it. The helmet had a chin strap. And a long cord with a plug at the end. Attached to the cord was a small metal box with a dial and an OFF/ON switch.

"It's a time-travel helmet." Marvin pointed to the dial with years stamped into the metal. "The pointer is on nineteen fifty-seven. Somebody came here from the future with this."

He turned it over.

Shanna saw tiny letters. They said MADE IN HONOLULU, U.S.A.

"So it was made in Hawaii," she said. "So what?"

"So," Marvin said. "Hawaii isn't one of the forty-eight states. It isn't part of the U.S.A. At least not now, in nineteen fifty-seven."

"But it will be!" Shanna grabbed the helmet. "Hawaii and Alaska didn't become states until . . ." She wished she'd paid more attention in her history class. "Around nineteen fifty-nine."

Shanna stared at the helmet in the fading daylight. This was it. Her ticket back to her home, her life.

She swallowed. Then she handed the helmet back to Marvin. "How does it work?" she asked.

Marvin grinned, showing his big teeth. "Allow me," he said.

Marvin set the dial for the proper year. Then he placed the helmet on Shanna's head and buckled the chin strap. He plugged in the cord. "Ready?" he asked.

Shanna hoped Marvin wasn't going to fry her brains out with this thing. She hoped he knew what he was doing. But really, she had no choice.

Either she stayed in 1957. Or she trusted Marvin.

Shanna swallowed again. Then she whispered, "Ready."

Marvin pushed the switch. Sparks flew from the switch box.

"No!" Shanna cried. "Wait!"

The last sound she heard was her own screaming.

Then — *WHOOSH!*

Shanna opened her eyes. She was sitting alone in a shed. On her head was a strange metal helmet.

She checked her watch. Still five-thirty. But, hey! Her watch was running again!

Was she home? Had she really made it back?

Shanna flung off the helmet. She opened the shed door and ran to her new house. She was panting hard by the time she got there. She slipped inside and hurried toward her room.

A boy stood at the end of the hall.

"David! Is that really you?" She gave him a big hug.

"Yuck!" David cried, pushing her away.

It was her brother, all right. She was home!

She ran into her room. Yes! Everything was just as she had left it. Her suitcase lay open on her bed. No frilly curtains. No bedspread. No Elvis pillow!

Shanna jumped up and down. She'd never felt so happy!

"Shanna?" her mom called. "Ready to go to Aunt Gigi's?"

"Okay!" Shanna called. Going to Aunt Gigi's suddenly didn't seem so bad.

As Shanna headed for the door, she glanced in the mirror.

She froze.

She still had on the powder-blue skirt and matching blouse!

And . . . her *hair*! Those awful little bangs! Still there.

Still there!

The next morning, Shanna woke up at five. She jumped into the shower and shampooed her hair. Then she put in the super-conditioning treatment.

Next, she worked with the blow-dryer. And

the hot rollers. She put on mousse. Gel. Hair spray.

At five of eight, her mom started calling from the kitchen.

But Shanna didn't answer. She stared into the mirror. Stared in horror.

It looked as if some little animal had gnawed off her bangs. Only worse. They poked out from her forehead. They wouldn't lie flat!

No way! *No way* she could start Westwood Middle School looking like this! It was too horrible to think about! She'd rather die!

Shanna yanked open a drawer, searching for her comb.

And saw the Cat Woman glasses with the rhinestone frames.

Shanna glanced into the mirror once more. And thought hard. . . .

The fifties were bad. But *anything* was better than starting a new school looking like a complete and total freak! *Anything!*

Shanna reached into the drawer and picked up the glasses. She slipped them on.

Then she shut her eyes and waited for the tingling to start.

MIRROR, MIRROR ON THE WALL

I have to be honest. I'm the prettiest girl in the entire sixth grade. No. More than that. I'm the prettiest twelve year old in all of Mill City.

At least I used to be.

I used to spend hours gazing at my mirror. Hours doing my hair. Trying on clothes. Making sure I looked perfect.

And then it happened. The thing that changed my life. Now the whole world is topsy-turvy, and everything is different.

I'm different.

What made me so pretty back then? I kept a list on the first page of my history notebook:

1. Thick, wavy blond hair
2. Blue eyes to die for
3. The sweetest button nose
4. Baby-soft skin
5. The straightest, whitest teeth

That was me. Bonnie Sue Bowers. No wonder I spent so much time in front of mirrors!

One afternoon, I stood in front of my bedroom mirror. "Who's the prettiest girl in Mill City?" I asked my reflection. Then I laughed out loud. I already knew the answer.

I tossed back my shiny, blond hair. I watched my dazzling smile light up my entire face.

Then I checked the calendar. I kept it taped to my floor-to-ceiling mirror.

"Let's see," I said, running my fingers along the dates. "Today is Saturday."

Mall day, of course.

I smoothed down my brand-new skirt. It was baby blue just like my eyes. Soft, rustling pleats swirled around my legs. I twirled around in a slow circle.

The Bonnie Sue in the mirror twirled too. And the pleats fluttered like feathers.

I brushed my hair, then flossed my teeth. I didn't take my eyes off the mirror for a second. "Perfect," I told my reflection.

"Hey, dog-face!" my brother, Ricky, shouted from the doorway. "Why are you always gawking at your dumb reflection?"

Ricky is eight years old, and a giant pain.

That day his greasy brown hair hung over his face. His hands were grimy with dirt. He'd been out wrestling with his friends in the mud again.

Of course I ignored him. That pest always calls me names. Dog-face. Mouse-breath. He thinks he's such a riot.

Ricky strode into my room. He held out his grubby hands. Then he edged closer to me, a grin on his face.

"I'm going to get you!" he teased. "I'm going to get you dirty!"

I leaped away — and started to shriek. "No! Noooo — get away from me!"

I stopped shrieking when I caught my reflection in the mirror.

Whoa! What is going on? I wondered.

The Bonnie Sue in the mirror was standing still with her mouth clamped shut!

How could that be?

How could my reflection not follow my every move? Was I seeing things?

I blinked in surprise, then took another look. The mouth in the mirror hung open just like mine.

I shrugged, and so did my reflection.

Okay, I thought. Back to normal.

"Ha!" Ricky cried. And he wiped his gross, filthy hands down the back of my shirt.

"You creep!" I screamed.

I leaned closer to the mirror for a better look. Long, brown mud smears trailed from my collar to my waist. One of my favorite outfits was ruined!

I went running to the stairs. "Mom!" I called. "Ricky got mud all over me!"

"Ricky, come down here right now," my mother called from the living room. "Leave your sister alone."

Ricky made a face and left. And I changed into an even cooler outfit for my trip to the mall.

Too bad nobody was there to see it. My friends were all away at summer camp or at the beach.

But I didn't really care. I needed to shop.

First I bought a sleek new swimsuit at The Clothes Closet. Then I went into Just Jeans and tried on two denim skirts, one black, one blue. I looked great in both colors.

I decided to get them. But before I left the fitting room, I took one last glance at the mirror.

I smiled at my reflection.

And my reflection stuck out her tongue!

I jumped back from the mirror. This couldn't be happening!

A reflection can't have a mind of its own! That's impossible!

I gasped.

My reflection gasped.

I shook my head.

So did my reflection.

Maybe I was seeing things. Or even worse — maybe I needed glasses!

I scooted closer to the mirror. I tossed my hair. I stamped my feet. I sighed.

My reflection followed my every move.

111

I was about to practice my beauty pageant walk in front of the mirror — when something pinched me. Hard!

I spun around in time to see . . .

No! It couldn't be.

But it was!

My reflection's hand — reaching out of the mirror to pinch me!

"Ohhhh," I moaned. This was for real. I wasn't seeing things! My reflection was *alive*!

My heart thudded wildly. I didn't know what to do. What to think. My knees gave way. I crumpled to the floor.

The room began to spin. I closed my eyes to shut out the light. To shut out my reflection.

I had to get home. Now!

I staggered to my feet. Then I grabbed my pocketbook and ran. Out of the fitting room. Away from the mirrors. I left the skirts.

I just wanted to be home.

I raced outside, then down the block. I broke out in a sweat. Imagine. Me — Bonnie Sue Bowers — sweating and running down the street!

"Hey! Disgusto!" Ricky called from the backyard. "What's your hurry?"

I didn't answer. I had to get to my room. My nice, safe room.

I pounded up the stairs to my bedroom. Finally! I slammed the door shut.

I tiptoed past the mirror. I tried to go by without looking. But I couldn't. I had to peek.

My reflection peeked back.

"You're in for it now!" she whispered fiercely.

Huh? She could *talk* too?

I jerked away, my body stiff with terror. I was too scared to scream. Too scared to do anything but back away.

I edged closer to the door. But I stumbled over my backpack and fell to my knees.

"Ha-ha-ha!" I heard my reflection's nasty laugh.

I jumped up quickly. I had to get away. Now! Before she reached for me again. I dove for the door.

"Where do you think you're going?" my reflection cried.

I didn't reply. I reached for the doorknob. But then I heard a *POP*.

I turned in time to see her head burst out of the mirror.

Another *pop*. Her shoulders sprang out.

POP! POP! POP! Her arms and legs stepped out from the glass. As I stared in shock, she leaped between me and the door. "Got you!" she cried.

With a frightened gasp, I shrank back. But there was nowhere to hide. Nowhere to go.

"Wh-what do you want?" I stammered.

"I'm taking over," my reflection replied — in *my voice*. "I'm tired of brushing my hair a million times a day. I'm tired of working so hard to look perfect."

She glared angrily at me. "And I'm tired of staring at *you* all day. I want a change. I want out. You're history, Bonnie Sue. *I'm* the real Bonnie Sue now."

The reflection grabbed my arm. She felt real. Solid. More than solid. Iron fingers gripped me tight.

I pulled back. But I couldn't break her hold! "Let me go!" I wailed.

"No way!" she snarled. "*You're* going inside the mirror now!"

"No! No! Please!" I struggled to get loose. I tried to pry her fingers off my arm.

But she dug her nails into my skin — perfectly manicured nails with bright red polish. *My* nails!

I was fighting *myself*. And *losing*!

It was all too much! I sank to the carpet.

But the reflection pulled me up. She pushed me to the mirror. My back pressed against the glass. It felt cold and hard.

A shiver ran through my body. She started to push me inside!

Do something, Bonnie Sue! I urged myself. Do something — now!

Weapon! I needed a weapon. I reached over my

reflection's shoulder — and grabbed my desk lamp.

With a desperate groan, I swung the lamp at my reflection.

Missed.

"Ohhh!" I cried out as the lamp smashed into the mirror.

"Noooooo!" I heard my reflection's horrified cry.

The mirror exploded. A million pieces of jagged glass shot through the air.

I ducked — and shielded my head with my arms.

Then, slowly, carefully, I raised my head and gazed around.

Was I safe? Was my reflection still there?

No.

She had vanished.

I took a deep breath, then slowly let it out. The whole crazy thing was over. Finished.

I had won! I had defeated her!

A smile spread across my face as I stepped over the shards of mirror on the floor. But my smile quickly died.

I could still see my reflection. There. And there. And there. And there. Reflected in each jagged piece of broken mirror.

My reflection sneered up at me. Grinning. As if *she* had won after all.

I gazed from piece to piece. I saw Bonnie Sue after Bonnie Sue. Dozens upon dozens of Bonnie Sues. Inside the broken pieces of mirror. Each one pointing a finger up at me.

I screamed.

Footsteps pounded up the stairs. "Bonnie Sue?" my mom called. "Are you okay?"

"In here, Mom!" I cried. "Help me!"

"There's no help for you!" dozens of voices called out. The reflections all spoke together.

And then, as I gaped in horror, they began to rise up.

Dozens of reflections! They floated up from the mirror pieces like ghosts.

Then they stood solidly on the floor. Bonnie Sues all around me, grinning, pointing, surrounding me. Dozens and dozens of me!

They pressed in tight. I couldn't move. Couldn't get away.

"Bonnie Sue?" My mother flung open the door. Ricky poked his head in behind her.

"What's going on here?" Mom shrieked.

"My reflections — they escaped from the mirror!" I cried.

"My reflections — they escaped from the mirror," all the other Bonnie Sues repeated together.

Ricky gasped. "Look at them all!" he exclaimed.

"Bonnie Sue — which one *are* you?" my mother demanded.

116

"I am!" I cried.

"I am!" cried all the Bonnie Sues.

I'm doomed! I thought. We all sound the same. And look the same. We're exactly alike.

How can I ever prove that I'm the real Bonnie Sue?

Then it hit me. *They* were all reflections. *I* was real. Maybe they wouldn't have reflections of their own.

It was worth a shot.

I fumbled through my backpack for the small mirror in my compact. Yes! My hand wrapped around it. I drew it out quickly.

Then I held it in front of me. My reflection was there for all to see.

"Mom — see?" I cried. "I have a reflection! Because I'm the real Bonnie Sue!"

I waved the glass in front of the other Bonnie Sues. The mirror didn't reflect a thing. No reflections.

"See?" I cried. "They don't have reflections — because they *are* reflections!"

"Bonnie Sue!" Mom cried happily. She pushed the others out of the way and hugged me.

And as she hugged me, I heard a long, terrifying howl.

I stared over Mom's shoulder — and saw the other Bonnie Sues all screaming and waving their hands over their heads.

Then something . . . some force . . . began

stretching them . . . pulling them off the floor. Into the air.

My little pocket mirror sucked them inside like a vacuum cleaner. One by one, they melted into a single reflection in my little round mirror.

When they all had disappeared, I raised the mirror to my face. I winked. My reflection winked. I tossed my hair. She tossed her hair.

"All right!" I cried in triumph.

I had defeated the reflections. Those copycats would never bother me again!

I hugged Mom again. I was so happy, I even hugged Ricky.

Then all three of us got to work, cleaning up the mess.

Now I didn't have a mirror in my room. But I didn't care. I could use the mirror in the bath-room.

That night, I decided to try a new hairstyle. I pinned my hair up. Then I stepped up to the bath-room mirror to brush it out.

I leaned close to the mirror. My reflection leaned toward me.

And grabbed me by the shoulders!

"Surprise!" she hissed. "You can't defeat me so easily. I've waited twelve years for this, Bonnie Sue!"

With a hard tug, she pulled me into the mirror.

Then she jumped out.

I stared at her from inside the glass. It was cold on this side of the mirror. My skin tingled. The air felt heavy and dry.

My reflection grinned at me. I grinned back at her.

She winked. I winked.

I'm a reflection now, I realized.

I've been a reflection ever since.

I'm waiting for my turn to climb back out. In the meantime, I do everything the new Bonnie Sue does. That's my job — right?

I only wish she would brush her hair once in a while. And put on a little lip gloss. And do her nails.

And why does she wear only torn jeans and enormous T-shirts?

Yuck! She's such a slob.

And that means that I'm a slob too.

I told you I've changed. I look just like her. It's so sad. . . .

If I were you, I'd stay away from mirrors.

Know what I mean?

WHAT'S COOKING?

My story starts in the year 1947.

That year, the cafeteria cook at the Mill Road School presented a new "Mystery Meat" every day. The cook's name was Susan Chopman. Each morning Susan Chopman left school with her cleaver and then returned with a bag of meat.

It was always gross. Slimy in one part, gristly in another. The kids nicknamed her Chop Suey because her "Chinese Surprise" was the worst lunch of all.

Then came the day of the chopped fingers. She *said* it was hot dogs in tomato soup. But the kids refused to eat it. They believed it was really chopped fingers.

They revolted, chanting, "Chop Suey! Chop Suey! Chop Suey!" It drove the cook wild. She flew into the lunchroom, hacking at tables with her meat cleaver, until the police dragged her out.

Years later, someone saw an obituary saying Susan Chopman was dead. Everyone said she had fallen on her own beloved cleaver while working in a meatpacking plant.

That's when the strange things began happening.

The cleaver marks on the walls. The hacked-up rats in the school refrigerator. The run-away school bus.

After that, they closed the school for good. . . .

"Cool story, Robert," Diana said as we came near the Mill Road School. Diana and I peered over the tall weeds and grass. The school was a square, three-story, brown-brick building. It had been boarded up for years.

Diana and I are cousins and neighbors. Friends too. This summer we had another thing in common. We'd both flunked math and were doomed to summer school at the old Mill Road School.

They were reopening it to deal with over-crowding in our school. But it wasn't quite ready yet.

Diana brushed aside the brown bangs of her short hair. "You have the greatest imagination, Robert," she said. "I love the stories you make up."

"But I didn't make this one up!" I cried. "Everyone in town knows the story of Chop Suey. Besides, I don't have a great imagination anymore. I've given that up."

"You can't give up an imagination," she scoffed.

"I'm going to," I insisted firmly.

At the end of school in June, the class voted me Most Imaginative. I was so embarrassed. Why couldn't I have been Most Athletic? Or Best Looking? (I have short blond hair and blue eyes. I don't think I'm bad looking.)

"Well, it's an awesome story," Diana said as we continued on to school. "They should make a movie of it."

Diana is a total movie fan. She's like a walking encyclopedia of movie facts.

"It's a cool story. But I didn't make it up," I insisted.

"Hey! Wait a minute!" Diana replied. "You're right! I have heard that story before. My friend Kevin told it to me. He says if you say 'Chop Suey' three times while standing on tiptoe, she'll come back from the dead. Can you imagine that?"

"No," I said scornfully. "I don't imagine anymore."

We stepped inside the old school. Workmen were everywhere — fixing windows, patching walls, repairing tiles.

Kids wandered around, not knowing where to go.

"Get to class," a teacher said, rushing down the hall.

"Where is our class?" I called after her. "We

have no idea." Too late. She was too far away to hear me. We walked down the hall, looking for a sign or something to tell us where to go.

We turned through a wide doorway. "Wow!" Diana said. "We found the lunchroom." Chop Suey's lunchroom.

It was pretty ordinary. Beat-up tables. Scuffed floor.

"Let's check out the kitchen where Chop Suey worked," Diana suggested.

The old kitchen stood behind a dust-covered door. The thrilled look on Diana's face worried me. "I'm going to say it," she told me. "I just have to."

"Go ahead," I replied. "Nothing will happen."

"We'll see," Diana said with a giggle. She stood on her toes. "Chop Suey! Chop Suey!" she sang out. "Chop Suey!"

At the very moment she finished, every single faucet in the place turned on — full blast.

Diana and I exchanged quick, startled glances. Then we raced out of the kitchen at full speed.

As I slid out into the hall, I turned to Diana.

She wasn't there! Where could she have gone?

Did Chop Suey get her?

No. No way! I told myself. That's my imagination again. Calm down, Robert. Be reasonable. But . . .

I grabbed the arm of a worker who was about to enter the lunchroom. "My friend . . . she's . . . ,"

I stammered, too scared to talk straight. "Chop Suey got her!"

We hurried inside. Diana lay sprawled on the floor. She'd slipped on some grease on the floor. "Chop Suey! She's in here!" she gasped.

"Yeah, sure," the worker said, rolling his eyes.

We followed him into the kitchen. He began turning off all the faucets. "I called her name three times — and the water just spurted out," Diana told him. "It's Chop Suey!"

"Is that old story still around?" the man asked, chuckling. "The faucets came on because I just opened the main water valve in the basement. I'm the plumber."

"Oh," Diana and I said in small, embarrassed voices.

We left the kitchen and continued searching. Finally, we found a sign directing us to our math class.

That first class was easy. Review stuff. Afterwards, we went out to the school yard to sit down for lunch.

"That plumber thought we were real jerks," I said, sitting cross-legged on the grass. "Talk about imagining things. See the trouble it causes?"

Diana settled down beside me. "I thought Chop Suey was going to fly out of that kitchen and chop me up," she admitted.

She made a disgusted face at the sandwich she

was unwrapping. "Mom gave me ham. I hate ham."

I offered her half of my peanut butter-and-jelly sandwich. But the moment I sank my teeth into my half, I knew something was wrong. Horribly wrong.

The peanut butter must have been a thousand years old! It felt slimy and wet. It tasted disgusting. I had to get rid of it before I puked. I jumped up and spat it out.

Diana was next to me, spitting out her half of the sandwich and gagging. She peeled apart the bread. "It's . . . it's liver!" she moaned. "*Raw* liver! Has your mother gone crazy?"

"I . . . I saw her make it," I sputtered. "She made PB and J. Someone switched my sandwich!" Diana and I both stared in shock at our sandwiches.

"Do you think Chop Suey did this? Maybe I really called her back from the dead," Diana murmured in a frightened voice.

"No way. It has to be somebody's idea of a sick joke," I insisted. I'd let my imagination go wild once today — I wasn't about to do it again.

That afternoon, I took out my books, shut my locker, and turned to Diana. "Ready to go?"

She stood there, totally frozen, with her back to me. Her shoulders were hunched, tense and stiff. "What's the matter?" I asked.

Diana turned and held out her blue backpack. Or, at least something that had once been her backpack. It was now just shredded blue strips of canvas.

"S-s-someone chopped this up," Diana uttered. "Someone with a . . . cleaver."

We gaped at the shredded bag. "Robert, it's true. She's back," Diana whispered. "First the sandwich, then this!"

Fighting panic, I thought hard. "There's probably just some sicko kid running around trying to scare kids. Let's not get crazy. Other kids know that story."

"I hope you're right," Diana said. "Should we tell the principal or someone?"

"I suppose so," I agreed. We walked to the principal's office. But it was dark and locked. "Oh, well. We can try tomorrow," I said. We walked out the front door together.

I kept staring at Diana's shredded backpack. How did that happen?

The next day, the lunchroom was scheduled to open for hot lunch. Diana and I were first on line with our trays. "Wouldn't it be weird if we really saw Chop Suey?" I said.

"You're using your imagination again," Diana teased.

"You're right," I admitted. "Sorry. But I know that —"

I was cut off by the sound of Diana's tray crashing to the floor. Her mouth dropped open. Her eyes goggled.

Behind the lunch counter stood the cook. A huge woman — at least six feet tall. With wild, black eyes. And a scowl on her round face.

In her hand she held a shining cleaver.

Diana squeezed my arm. "It's — *her!*"

The woman laughed. "I forgot to put the cleaver down," she said. She set the blade aside and patted it fondly. "Step up for a yummy lunch, children."

Diana and I stared at her without moving.

"Come along," the woman cooed.

Slowly, we slid our trays along the counter, closer to her.

The woman pushed a bowl of tomato soup with hot dog pieces toward me. "Tomato Soup Surprise," she announced.

My mouth dropped open. I stared down at the bubbling soup.

"What's wrong?" she barked. "Don't you like tomato soup and hot dogs?"

"We love it," Diana said quickly. She grabbed a bowl of soup from the counter and placed it on her tray.

"Everyone loves Aunt Sue's cooking," the woman crooned.

"Aunt *Sue!*" Diana gasped. We made our way to the nearest table. "Aunt Sue Chopman! It's her. I told you!"

"Her name just happens to be Sue, and this is just soup," I said, trying to keep calm.

At the table, we stared into the soup. The swirling hot dog pieces were a dull gray.

"I'm not eating this," Diana said firmly. "What if it's rat meat . . . or worse?"

I poked one of the hot dog pieces with my spoon. Yuck. Diana and I both pushed away our bowls.

On the way out, Diana gripped my arm. "Look at tomorrow's menu," she said, gasping. Written on a blackboard in wild, loopy script were the words: TOMORROW'S LUNCH — MEAT SURPRISE! AUNT SUE'S SPECIAL RECIPE.

"She's staring at us," Diana whispered.

I turned from the menu board. Aunt Sue stood behind the lunch counter, her big arms tightly folded. She glared hard at Diana and me.

"Let's go," I told Diana. My heart hammered.

"Diana! We have to stop this!" I insisted, out in the hall. "We're driving ourselves crazy. It's nuts."

"It's not crazy!" Diana replied. "It's her. We called her. So she's after us. We're the ones who called her back from the dead!"

"We?" I yelped. "I didn't call her. *You* did."

"You were with me. I guess that counts."

"Oh, great," I said, rolling my eyes. "But it doesn't matter. Because she's not Chop Suey. She's just a wacky old cafeteria cook."

After school, Diana and I were almost home —

when Diana stopped. She unzipped her new backpack and looked inside. "I forgot my math book. And we have a test tomorrow."

Her face went pale. "I think I left it in the lunchroom. Forget it. I'll fail. No way am I going back in there!"

"Come on," I told her, turning back. "Let's go get it." I felt really proud of myself for being so calm and brave.

The front door to the old school was locked. "Everybody's gone," I said. "Maybe there's an open door in back."

Sure enough, we found one of the back doors open. We went in and sneaked past the classroom where a whistling janitor was busy mopping the floor.

We stepped into the silent lunchroom and glanced around.

The big room was empty. Diana's math book was on a table near the door. She grabbed it, and we turned to leave.

"See?" I told her. "There was nothing to — "

"Not so fast," a voice snarled.

We froze.

Aunt Sue stood in the doorway. Her cleaver gleamed in her hand. "So, you don't like Aunt Sue's Tomato Surprise?" she growled.

We stepped back. Diana gripped my wrist. "We loved it!" she told the woman.

"Liar!" she screamed, lumbering toward us.

Her eyes shone with rage. "I saw you. You didn't eat it!"

Swinging her cleaver over her head, she dove at us.

Diana and I darted behind a table.

With a wild war cry, Aunt Sue arched her back and heaved the cleaver over her head.

The blade of her cleaver crashed into the table-top.

Aunt Sue raced to the table. She yanked at the cleaver furiously.

"Come on!" I cried, pulling Diana with me toward the door.

We raced into the nearest classroom and slammed the door behind us. Frantically, Diana turned the bolt lock. Our backs against the door, we panted hard.

"Oh, boy! Oh, boy! Oh, boy!" was all I could manage to say.

"We've got to get rid of her," Diana gasped. "There has to be a way. There's always a way in the movies."

I gripped Diana's arm. My other hand shook as I pointed to the window.

Aunt Sue—Chop Suey—was floating out there!

Floating in the air and laughing.

Screaming, we fumbled with the lock.

But it was jammed.

Chop Suey flew into the classroom.

"We're dead meat!" I cried.

"That's right. You're tomorrow's Meat Surprise!" Chop Suey screamed with delight.

We were cornered. No way out!

Diana thought out loud as she pounded the lock. "I saw a movie where they said the monster's name backwards, and — "

Diana stopped as Chop Suey floated toward us, her cleaver held high over her head.

"Split up. She can't get both of us at once!" I screamed.

Diana ran in one direction. I went the other way.

Chop Suey floated toward me.

I scrambled onto the teacher's desk — as her cleaver sliced the air. Chop Suey grinned. "Got you now!" she cried.

"Hey, Chop Suey!" Diana called from the window.

Chop Suey whirled around angrily. "Don't call me that!" she shrieked. She raised the cleaver above her head and roared toward Diana.

I stared in horror. Diana's eyes met mine.

"Let's try that backwards movie idea," Diana called.

I nodded okay.

"Suey Chop! Suey Chop! Suey Chop!" we shouted desperately. "Go away!"

Chop Suey's mouth dropped open in surprise. "Noooooo!" She let out a long, horrified howl. Then she began spinning around the room as if she were caught in a tornado.

Her cleaver flew out of her hand. It flipped through the air — and wedged itself into the blackboard behind me.

When I looked up again, Chop Suey had vanished.

"It worked!" Diana cried happily. "It worked, Robert! Just like in the movie!"

"Let's get out of here!" I cried. "Summer school is over!"

I ran home and found Mom in the kitchen. "Mom, wait until I tell you what happened!" I exclaimed.

"Can you tell me later?" she asked. "I'm late for a meeting right now. Listen, I ordered from the Chinese restaurant. You weren't here, so I ordered *lo mein* for you. Okay?"

"What else did you order?" I asked, suddenly realizing I was starving.

"Oh, you know your father," she said, standing on her toes and reaching for a bowl in the cabinet. "He always orders the same thing. Every single time. Chop Suey! Chop Suey! Chop —"

"Mom — *no!*" I screamed.

"Suey . . . What's the matter, Robert?"

Before I could answer, the doorbell rang.

"That's probably the delivery person," she said. "Would you answer the door, please, Robert?"

ABOUT R. L. STINE

R.L. Stine is the most popular author in America. He is the creator of the *Goosebumps, Give Yourself Goosebumps, Fear Street,* and *Ghosts of Fear Street* series, among other popular books. He has written more than 100 scary novels for kids. Bob lives in New York City with his wife, Jane, teenage son, Matt, and dog, Nadine.

GET
Goosebumps®
by R.L. Stine

☐ BAB45365-3	#1	Welcome to Dead House	$3.99
☐ BAB45369-6	#5	The Curse of the Mummy's Tomb	$3.99
☐ BAB49445-7	#10	The Ghost Next Door	$3.99
☐ BAB49450-3	#15	You Can't Scare Me!	$3.99
☐ BAB47742-0	#20	The Scarecrow Walks at Midnight	$3.99
☐ BAB48355-2	#25	Attack of the Mutant	$3.99
☐ BAB48348-X	#30	It Came from Beneath the Sink	$3.99
☐ BAB48349-8	#31	The Night of the Living Dummy II	$3.99
☐ BAB48344-7	#32	The Barking Ghost	$3.99
☐ BAB48345-5	#33	The Horror at Camp Jellyjam	$3.99
☐ BAB48346-3	#34	Revenge of the Lawn Gnomes	$3.99
☐ BAB48340-4	#35	A Shocker on Shock Street	$3.99
☐ BAB56873-6	#36	The Haunted Mask II	$3.99
☐ BAB56874-4	#37	The Headless Ghost	$3.99
☐ BAB56875-2	#38	The Abominable Snowman of Pasadena	$3.99
☐ BAB56876-0	#39	How I Got My Shrunken Head	$3.99
☐ BAB56877-9	#40	Night of the Living Dummy III	$3.99
☐ BAB56878-7	#41	Bad Hare Day	$3.99
☐ BAB56879-5	#42	Egg Monsters from Mars	$3.99
☐ BAB56880-9	#43	The Beast from the East	$3.99
☐ BAB56881-7	#44	Say Cheese and Die–Again!	$3.99
☐ BAB56882-5	#45	Ghost Camp	$3.99
☐ BAB56883-3	#46	How to Kill a Monster	$3.99
☐ BAB56884-1	#47	Legend of the Lost Legend	$3.99
☐ BAB56885-X	#48	Attack of the Jack-O'-Lanterns	$3.99
☐ BAB56886-8	#49	Vampire Breath	$3.99
☐ BAB56887-6	#50	Calling All Creeps	$3.99
☐ BAB56888-4	#51	Beware, the Snowman	$3.99

Scare me, thrill me, mail me GOOSEBUMPS now!

Available wherever you buy books, or use this order form. Scholastic Inc., P.O. Box 7502,
2931 East McCarty Street, Jefferson City, MO 65102

Please send me the books I have checked above. I am enclosing $_____ (please add $2.00 to cover shipping and handling). Send check or money order — no cash or C.O.D.s please.

Name _____ Age _____

Address _____

City _____ State/Zip _____

Please allow four to six weeks for delivery. Offer good in the U.S. only. Sorry,
mail orders are not available to residents of Canada. Prices subject to change.

Hey Goosebumps fans!
Don't write this one off!

Boo dudes!
More greetings from the world of Goosebumps!
I've got a brand-new
collection of 30 totally
terrifying cards in The
Goosebumps® Postcard Book II —
with a different, scary Goosebumps
cover on the front of each one!

Collect 'em, swap 'em,
or send them to your
favorite monster.
Yours ghoully,
Curly

TO:

The
Goosebumps®
Postcard Book II
Coming this April to a bookstore near you.

Last one in's
a rotten...ghost!

Goosebumps®

Sarah hates Camp Cold Lake. It's a
water sports camp, and Sarah hates
the outdoors. Worst of all, nobody
wants to be her swimming buddy.
Nobody, that is, but Della. Too bad
Della's a ghost....

The Curse of
Camp Cold Lake

Goosebumps #56

R.L. Stine

Floating in a bookstore near you!

GBT1096

R.L. STINE

Goosebumps®

PRESENTS

TV BOOK #13

Jerry can't wait to explore the dark, old cave he found down at the beach. The other kids are too scared to go in — they say the cave is haunted! But Jerry knows there's no such thing as ghosts. Right?

**Goosebumps Presents
TV Book #13**

GHOST BEACH

by R.L. Stine

With 8 pages of full-color photos from the show!

Look for it in a bookstore near you!